KILL PATTON!

KILL PATTON!

Leo Kessler

This first world edition published in Great Britain 2003 by
SEVERN HOUSE PUBLISHERS LTD of
9–15 High Street, Sutton, Surrey SM1 1DF.
This first world edition published in the USA 2003 by
SEVERN HOUSE PUBLISHERS INC of
595 Madison Avenue, New York, N.Y. 10022.

British Library Cataloguing in Publication Data

Kessler, Leo, 1926-
  Kill Patton!
  1.   Patton, George S. (George Smith), 1885-1945 - Fiction
  2.   World War, 1939-1945 - Campaigns - Italy - Sicily - Fiction
  3.   War stories
  I.   Title
  823.9'14 [F]

ISBN 0-7278-6000-3

Typeset by Palimpsest Book Production Ltd.,
Polmont, Stirlingshire, Scotland.
Printed and bound in Great Britain by
MPG Books Ltd., Bodmin, Cornwall.

PRELUDE:
A Murder is Proposed

The first Mitchell bomber hit the runway with a loud thud. One tyre burst immediately. The bomber's mad dash across the cratered Sicilian runway came to an abrupt, frightening stop. It skidded and shimmied violently to the left as the desperate pilot tried to retain control. There was the ear-splitting sound of metal rending. An instant later the undercarriage collapsed. The twin-engined US plane slammed to the tarmac in a cloud of dust and flying metal. Frantically the crew started to drop out of the wrecked fuselage, as the first greedy red flames began to lick up from the fractured gas tanks. In a moment the Mitchell would explode.

'*General*!' Colonel Codman grabbed his boss just in time. At the end of the runway the fire truck roared into action. The air was full of its sirens sounding their urgent warning. '*No, you can't help*,' Codman yelled above the racket.

'But goddamit—' General Patton began. The rest of his outburst was drowned by the gas tanks exploding. Searing red flame like a gigantic blowtorch roared the length of the fuselage. The blast whipped the observer's face, as if by a blow from a flabby fist.

Shielding his face from the heat of the burning bomber, General Patton's aide pulled the ex-Seventh Army commander back to relative safety as the rest of the group came straggling in from the sea, limping back to their Sicilian base the best they could. Codman, the ex-pilot, could see the raid had been a failure. The bomber group had been shot to pieces. Their formation was all to hell and the evening sky was full of Mitchells trailing smoke behind them, while others were wave-hopping, firing red distress flares to indicate that the crippled planes were carrying wounded. Indeed, Codman told himself that he'd be surprised if something *didn't* go wrong before they reached the coast and safety. They might have to ditch in the water yet.

It was obvious that the folk in the control tower thought the same. Ambulances were rushing out to meet the bombers already and green flares were soaring out into the darkening sky to tell the approaching pilots that all was clear; the runways were theirs.

Next to Codman, the immaculately uniformed general slapped his swagger cane against the side of his highly polished boot in a mixture of frustration and rage. 'Those brave boys,' he keened in that strange high-pitched voice of his, then immediately afterwards he snarled, 'Those goddamned air force types. Why do they send our guys out against the Krauts like that? Why, they're so damn dumb, they can't even fart and chew gum at the same time.'

On any other occasion, Codman would have chuckled in his respectful manner at the boss's profane outburst. Not now, however. The boss was in trouble enough already. 'Now, now, sir,' he said carefully. 'We're guests here, sir. We don't want any trouble with the Army Air Corps brass, do we sir?'

Patton sighed hard. 'Yes, I suppose you're right, Codman . . . Why, goddamit, Charley, you're always right. I guess if you'd have commanded the Seventh Army, you'd never have gotten yourself into such a mess like I goddam did . . .'

Codman had not been with the boss that fateful August 10th, 1943, when it had all started. Since then he had wished a dozen times a day that he had been. For if he had been, he was sure that he'd have prevented Patton from doing what he did, which had seemingly landed him permanently in the doghouse and had finally resulted in 'Ike'* taking Patton's beloved Seventh Army away from him.

That hot summer's day Patton had come upon the 93rd Evac Field Hospital just by chance. He had roared into the place, the siren of his command car howling, waving his fists above his head like the champion at the lightly wounded men waiting to have their wounds attended to. The men grinned back at him, half flattered, half amused at the sight of the commanding general, the legendary Patton. They might complain among themselves that George Patton had founded his fighting reputation on their 'blood' and his 'guts', hence his nickname 'Ole Blood an' Guts Patton'. But woe if any GI from another outfit criticized their commander. The fur would then fly – and how!

Now Patton put on one of his many faces – his 'seriously concerned for the welfare of his troops' one. Brushing aside the flap of one of the big tents filled with more gravely wounded men, he started to move from litter to litter, patting the wounded, indulging in the usual small talk that generals do when speaking to the men they had sent into battle, only for them to return broken, even dying.

He didn't get far, however. For now he came to a litter on which rested a young soldier whose body bore no sign of wounds – no bandages, no splints. Patton looked puzzled. 'What brought you here, son?' he asked kindly enough, though already his eyes were beginning to glint angrily, for he had guessed why this obviously unwounded soldier was here among all his 'heroes'.

'I'm running a fever, sir,' the soldier replied miserably.

---

*Ike, General Eisenhower, the Allied Supreme Commander.

'Yessir,' the nearest doctor in a bloodstained white overall chimed in. 'A little over one hundred and two.'

Patton raised his eyebrows. He was about to say something when he noticed another young GI squatting near the door morosely nursing a cigarette. 'And what's the goddam matter with you?' he snapped.

The man started to tremble immediately. His hand holding the Camel began to shake. 'It's my nerves,' he quavered.

'What did you say?' Patton rasped, his thin face flushing.

The GI began to sob. 'It's my nerves . . . I can't stand the shelling no more.'

Patton could contain himself no longer. He slapped his boot with his cane with a vicious whack. 'Your *nerves*! Christ on a crutch, you're just a goddam coward, you yellow son of a bitch!' He reached out and slapped the sobbing GI sharply across the face. Behind him the doctors sucked in their breath with shock. Patton didn't seem to notice. 'Shut up that goddam sobbing. I won't have these brave men who have been shot see a yellow bastard sitting there crying like a frigging baby that's wet its frigging diaper!' Before any of the shocked doctors could stop Patton, he reached out abruptly and gave the soldier a sharp blow. The man yelped. His helmet liner flew from his head into the next tent.

Patton didn't seem to notice. He swung round on the ashen-faced, shocked receiving officer and yelled into his face, 'Don't you dare admit this yellow son of a bitch. I won't have my hospitals cluttered up with these bastards who haven't got the guts to frigging well fight!'

He turned back to the man he had just struck. He had managed now to 'sit to attention', as was expected of an enlisted man in the presence of a senior officer, though he was still trembling violently. 'You, you bastard, are going back to the front line and you may get shot and killed there. But you're gonna frigging well fight. If you don't,' Patton's thin lips curled back in a wolfish grin which revealed his yellowing teeth, 'I'll stand you up against a wall and have a firing squad kill you on purpose.'

His chest heaving with the effort, Patton gasped for breath. Next moment his hand fell to his celebrated ivory-handled revolver. 'In fact, I ought to shoot you myself, you goddamned whimpering coward!'

'*Sir!*' the receiving officer yelled.

Patton caught himself just in time. His hand dropped from the handle of his .45 and he let himself be led out of the tent. But as he did so, he was still yelling about sending the 'yellow son of a bitch' back to the firing line, while everywhere female nurses, orderlies, doctors and lightly wounded men pushed forward in order to see the show.

Patton must have known then, Codman had rationalized afterwards when he first heard of the terrible event, that he had made an almost fatal mistake, for he had known instinctively that the head of the field hospital would have to make a report about an incident witnessed by so many people. But neither he nor his boss had realized that Patton had virtually cooked his goose.

By the end of the Allied campaign in Sicily, with both the Americans and British preparing to launch their attack over the Straits of Messina into Italy proper, the press had gotten hold of the incident and were threatening to publish details in the paper back in the States. For a while the military authorities, whose chief was Patton himself, had managed to sit on the incident using their powers of censorship. But after details came to light of a second slapping incident under the same circumstances as before, neither Patton nor Eisenhower were able to censor the details.

On the very same day that a triumphant Patton had entered Messina as a conquering hero and thus ended the campaign, a report had been flashed back to Washington, detailing what had happened as a suddenly gloomy Patton had blurted out, 'Now the shit really hits the fan!'

It had. For a while Eisenhower had tried to protect the Seventh Army commander, but when it appeared that he, too, was going to be in trouble if he continued to do so, Ike had let it go. For a day or two, Patton ate humble pie. He apologized to the two soldiers. He apologized to his army. He apologized to Eisenhower. He apologized to the press, the mothers of America. As he cursed to Codman, his loyal aide, 'Goddam, I'll even apologize to the Krauts if they want me to!'

But it was no use. All the apologies in the world would not get him off the hook now. By the end of November Patton had been dismissed from the command of his army. It went over the Straits to fight in Italy without the general who had created it. Instead Patton was left in his loud echoing palazzo in Sicily, deserted by most of his staff save for Colonel Codman – for they felt Patton's star had fallen and they had been eager to hitch themselves to a new one.

Now while Ike and his one-time subordinate, General Bradley, had headed for England to prepare for the great invasion of France, a gloomy – almost suicidal – 'Ole Blood an' Guts' had been abandoned here waiting for a new call to arms, which seemingly would never come. Instead he was given the minor role of a general commanding an invisible army which might be used in the Balkans to help the attack on what Churchill called Europe's 'soft underbelly'. 'Tough old gut', as the troops engaged in heavy fighting in Italy were already calling it. It was now Patton's assignment to tour the area and show himself so that the Germans would think he was being held in reserve for some new local battle.

'Even the Krauts can't be that nuts,' had been Patton's rueful comment on several occasions. 'A commander without an army! Who could be so damned dumb as to believe that!'

It was for that reason that Patton was here on this Sicilian bomber field that afternoon. He was to be photographed welcoming the Mitchell crews back after a successful raid on the German-held Italian naval ports further up the 'boot' of Italy. The pictures would appear in the US Army's newspaper, *The Stars & Stripes*, which the Germans would pick up and believe that the raids were intended to prepare for Patton's landing further up the coast – perhaps leading to a drive across Italy to Rome itself. After all, the Germans knew Patton as a dashing leader of such bold mobile raids.

Patton had come to the field this day reluctantly. 'Jesus H,' he had commented bitterly to Codman as they had ridden to the bomber field, 'Is that all I'm good for now? For this kind of baloney crap . . . Just a goddam ancient frigging decoy duck!'

But as the surviving planes came straggling in, smoke pouring from shattered engines, more and more red distress flares hissing into the sky over the field, Codman told himself that the US Army Signal Corps would not be taking any pictures of the general this December day. The field was in a mess, with shattered burning Mitchells everywhere and wounded young men lying on the bloodstained tarmac crying out for help. Even with Patton in the pictures, the army censors would never allow a scene of such carnage to be published in the papers back home. Codman shivered in spite of his thick greatcoat. It was time to go home to the gloomy palazzo and fill the general with as much bourbon as he could tolerate before he said his prayers and went to bed. Now all he, Codman, could do was to cheer his boss up a bit.

'Sir,' he called to where Patton was standing protectively. He was bending over a teenage gunner, his blond hair matted a bright red with his own blood, his remaining hand clutching the empty air, as if trying to hold on to life itself, his eyes rolled back, fish-white.

'*Give him air, for hell's sake!*' Patton was yelling angrily as the airmen attempted to crowd round. 'And get some coats over him . . . Keep him warm.' Frantically Patton struggled with his own expensive, custom-made jacket in order to threw it over the dying airman. But it was already too late. The kid's spine arched like a taut bow string. He gave a weird cry that seemed to come from the very depths of his being. For what seemed an eternity but which, in reality, was only a split second, the air gunner stayed like that. Then with a pitiful groan he collapsed back on the bloody tarmac, dead before he hit it.

Patton paused in his attempts to remove his jacket. Then he gently bent down, ignoring the blood and the gore and the severed arm that now lay foolishly near its dead owner, and closed the boy's eyelids, one after the other. Tears started to trickle down his stern face. He mumbled something then turned to Codman and said, voice thick with emotion, 'Codman, take me back to that damned palazzo of mine . . . I need a frigging drink.'

Despite the crudity of his expressions, Codman could see the boss was moved. Beneath that tough swagger of his, 'Ole Blood an' Guts' was a very sentimental, emotional man.

'Yessir!' Codman snapped, 'I'll have you back – er – home in two shakes of a lamb's tail.'

But General Patton was not fated to get back home that quickly this December day. Indeed, as Codman later reconstructed the events of what happened when they left the airfield with its dead and dying young aircrews, someone had intended that General Patton should never return to his 'home' in that loud echoing Sicilian palazzo ever again.

Deep in thought, Patton slumped in the back seat of his command car, no longer feeling it important to sit to attention as he had once done when he had been the conquering hero in Sicily. For now there were few GIs left on the island – they'd all gone to the new front in Italy and the 'Darkies', as Patton called the Service Corps blacks who still remained in Sicily, were seemingly unworthy of a fighting American soldier's attention. Here and there the ragged Sicilian peasants with skinny-ribbed donkeys took off their hats and stood humbly on the side of the dusty track as the car passed. But for the most part they hurriedly got out of the way. For by now they knew how impatient 'il Generale Patton' could be with anyone and anything that hindered his progress. Hadn't General Patton ordered during the campaign that the mules of a poor dirt farmer should be shot because they obstructed his passage over a bridge?

Now, as the light began to fade altogether, the command car started to edge its way into the outskirts of Palermo where Patton's palazzo was located. Suddenly the air was full of the scents and sounds of a typical Sicilian town in the evening: the pungent smell of garlic and cheap black tobacco, the sizzling of slabs of goat meat, the cries of the hawkers and the black-clad peasant women with their wickerwork baskets as they traded their fruit and other cheap wares, the honk of the ancient taxis which belched smoke or were propelled by huge billowing gas bags filled with coal gas, carried on makeshift trailers towed behind them. All was noise, cries, shouted greetings.

In an instant the lone command car was swamped by vehicles and people. The harassed GI corporal slowed down to a snail's pace. Now and again he pulled at the rope of the steamboat foghorn. The blast of sound had no effect. It was dissipated by the noises all around. Codman started to look worried. He wanted to have the general 'home' before Palermo was blacked out, for the Sicilians were notoriously careless and the undisguised lights, as poor as they were, invariably attracted low-level German bombers to the Sicilian capital. After all the boss had been through lately, Codman didn't want to have him injured or, God forbid, killed by some stray Kraut bomb. What an end that would be to Patton's glorious military career: killed in exile in an obscure part of southern Europe, which most Americans back home had never even heard of.

Codman dug his elbow into the harassed driver's ribs. 'Joe,' he urged, 'put some pep into it, willya? Make these wops move . . . Why the Sam Hill can't they get outa the way?'

The driver spat over the side of the car. 'They're wops, aren't they, Colonel sir,' he answered, as if that explained everything. Now they were moving at less than five miles an hour. It seemed to Codman that those dark Italian faces, hollow-cheeked, often toothless, and flashing-eyed, were pressing ever close to their vehicle. He told himself he could even smell the stink of their unwashed bodies. He felt nauseated and remembered the general had often maintained that the Siclians stank worse than those 'damned A-rabs', who he had come to hate with a passion in North Africa back in '42.

Up above them in the tall eighteenth-century houses, which looked as if they hadn't been painted since they were built, heavy-bosomed women, some with babies suckling at their big bosoms, were closing rickety shutters for the approaching blackout. Codman thought he caught a glimpse of a woman with her skirt thrown up over her back, while a skinny, sweating youth was humping her furiously. Codman allowed himself a momentary grin. At least someone was enjoying himself in this fetid sewer, he thought. Then his grin vanished as quickly as it had appeared. The car had come to a sudden stop.

He swung his gaze to the front. A few yards in front of them a mule, skinny ribbed and wasted, as they all were in Sicily, had slipped its load. Now it stood there, head bent in dismal resignation, while its angry owner, unusually fat and tall for a Sicilian, beat it cruelly with a nailed stick. Time and time again he thwacked what was really a hefty club down on the animal's shabby, patchy hide, raising blood every time, so that the mule's back looked as if it were covered with the loathsome symptoms of some awful skin disease.

Codman felt hot, sickening bile rise in his throat. God, how cruelly these wops treat their animals, he told himself. Yet at the same time he was angry – angry that the general was being forced to witness such unnecessary sadism. 'Holy cow, Joe,' he cursed. 'Can't you goddam do something to get us out of this mess?'

'I could shoot the mule?'

'Better to shoot the damned owner,' Codman retorted bitterly. 'He ought to have it coming—'

The rest of his words were drowned by a single sharp crack. It was like a dry twig snapping underfoot in the woods in a hot New England summer. Suddenly, startlingly, the windscreen in front of the driver shattered into a glittering spider's web of broken glass. Joe gave a soft groan. Slowly, but inevitably, his head fell towards the wheel. Codman's mouth dropped stupidly. Just beneath Joe's helmet liner a neat wrinkled red hole, rimmed with a black powder burn, had suddenly appeared. Someone in that darkening but packed Palermo square had just killed General Patton's driver!

SECTION ONE
Enter the Limeys

One

The Kiwis had taken the town now. Their leading infantry was already passing through the burning Italian town and heading for the open country beyond. Behind them they left panic, chaos and sudden, violent death. The buildings swayed and trembled like stage backdrops under the impact of the continued bombardment. Streams of panicked Italian refugees hurried through the burning streets, carrying their pathetic bundles on their heads, hobbling on crutches, pushing prams containing screaming infants.

To the right a woman lay writhing and screaming in agony. White pellets of phosphorus were imbedded in both her naked breasts. Now exposed to the air, the pellets had begun to burn fiercely, eating away the tender flesh. Next to her lay her dead baby, also sprawled naked in the filthy gutter.

'My God!' the New Zealand platoon commander gasped, his young bronzed face contorted and crazy. 'You can't believe such things possible! . . . Man couldn't do this to his fellow men! . . . No, *impossible*!' He turned to one side and, steadying himself against the bullet-pocked wall, began to retch violently.

The little, swarthy-faced intelligence sergeant, known as Campbell 175 to distinguish him from all the other Campbells in the British Army, was unmoved. He had seen worse, especially at the Battle of El Alamein, where he had suffered such a terrible wound that he had been

17

transferred from the Black Watch to the Intelligence Corps – something which had undoubtedly saved his life. For, as they had wise-cracked in the Highland Division, 'the only way to get outa the infantry, Jock, is in a wee box or feet first.'

Now he turned his gaze from the scene of horror in front of him to the line of prisoners, most of whom were German, though there were a few Italian blackshirt fascists among them. They leaned or slumped against the shattered wall. Several trembled like leaves. Others puffed nervously at the Woodbines and Victory cigarettes given to them by their captors. But a few of the Germans showed no emotion at all. Instead they stood there, stoically prepared to accept any fate the Tommies had in store for them.

Campbell 175's face grew grim. He knew the type. He'd seen enough of the blond bastards in his time, not only in the North African desert, but also in Germany before the war. He shot a glance at the young New Zealand officer. He was still vomiting, his shoulders heaving like those of a heartbroken child. He was no good, Campbell 175 told himself. He turned to the long, lean Kiwi corporal with the ribbon of the Africa Star on his blouse. He looked like a typical old sweat as he leaned there, smoking moodily but not taking his eye off the German prisoners for one instant. 'Corporal,' he commanded.

'Yes, Sarge?' The Kiwi didn't straighten up as a British NCO would have done when addressed by a superior.

'Get that big blond bugger with the stripes over here,' Campbell ordered.

The Kiwi nodded. He spat out his gasper and pointed his bayoneted rifle in the direction of the German soldier. 'All right, Adolf, move . . . yer wanted.'

The German looked at the New Zealander haughtily, rumpling his nose as if he had smelled something distinctly unpleasant. For a moment it looked as if he might not move.

But when the Kiwi pricked his side with the sharp bayonet, he moved all right.

Campbell 175 looked up at the German. 'SS?' he demanded.

'I no SS,' the German replied easily, looking down at the swarthy-faced sergeant somewhat contemptuously. '*Wehrmacht . . . I.*' He prodded his big chest with a dirty finger and spat on the ground at Campbell's feet, either to show his contempt of the SS or perhaps of the sergeant himself.

Campbell affected not to notice. Instead he rasped in perfect German, '*Los zieh' deine Jacke aus. Wollen mal sehen.*'

The German couldn't conceal his surprise. Perhaps he was too shocked by the fluent German to obey the order to remove his jacket. But the Kiwi corporal looked happy. He thought the German was disobeying the order the funny little English sergeant had just given the big man. 'Shall I tickle him with me tin opener, Sarge?' he asked eagerly. 'Only thing old Jerry understands – a bit o' steel up his jacksy.'

Campbell smiled softly. 'No, won't be necessary. He'll do as he's told, Corporal.' And then he bellowed, bringing his face as close as he could to that of the surprised German prisoner. '*Los, wirds bald, Mensch!*'

That did it. Swiftly the German pulled off his dirty tunic. An instant later he stood there, bare-armed and shivering a little without his jacket, perhaps because of the December cold or from fear of this strange, intense, little Tommy sergeant.

Campbell 175 seemingly had no time to waste. He snapped, '*Arme hoch – schnell!*' The prisoner's muscular arms shot up.

Nose wrinkled in distaste at the smell coming from the German's hairy unwashed armpits, the sergeant examined his inner arms for the giveaway sign. He found it almost immediately. Set against the white flesh of the man's arm, there it was – the tattooed blood group mark that only SS troopers carried. There was no denying. There it was – black against white. Blood group A.

Campbell allowed himself a little smile of triumph, but it was a smile that boded no good for the prisoner. He hadn't reckoned on the stupid Tommies knowing so much about the Waffen SS. His lips quavered. Suddenly he was afraid, very afraid, and all his former confident bluster vanished immediately. *'Nein . . . nein,'* he pleaded, face contorted and ashen with fear. *'Ich bin nicht bei der SS, Herr Unteroffizier . . . Glauben Sir mir—'*

'Schnauze!' Campbell cut him off sharply. To the now grinning corporal, he said, 'Can you escort the bastard round the back of this house. The other chap can look after 'im, eh?'

Behind them the young officer had recovered from his vomiting. He said thickly, wiping his mouth, 'What's going on, Sergeant?'

'This, sir. I'm going to shoot this Jerry.'

'Shoot him? But you can't shoot prisoners like that . . . out of hand. It's against the Geneva Convention,' he stuttered, his young face reflecting his astonishment.

'I can,' the little sergeant answered calmly. 'Before the Germans retreated, these SS set this place on fire and started blowing up the remaining buildings to make our advance more difficult than it bloody well was already.' He indicated the mountain peaks all around with a quick sweep of his hand. 'And the bastards are going to do the same with the next Eyetie village and the next if we let 'em get away with it.'

'But how are you going to do that by shooting—'

Campbell 175 didn't let the young New Zealand officer finish his question; there was no time to be wasted. 'I'm going to shoot another couple of 'em if I find the SS swine, and then that kid over there.' He indicated a youth who didn't look older than sixteen, nursing his bloodstained cheek bandage and looking very worried with it. 'He's SS too. Can you see the clear mark on his tunic where he's ripped off the SS armband?'

The officer nodded.

'Well I'm gonna let the young bugger run for it. You know – like you throw a fish that's too small back in the river.' He laughed cynically and so did the corporal. 'He'll get back to his unit and he'll tell his CO what those sadistic Tommies of the New Zealand Division do to the SS if they're captured. I have a feeling, sir, that after that this SS Battalion *Wotan* won't put up any more last ditch stands.'

'Good on you, mate,' the Kiwi corporal cried enthusiastically, as up front the sudden hysterical high-pitched burr of a German Spandau machine-gun indicated that the advancing Kiwis had already bumped into fresh German resistance.

'But . . .' the young officer began to protest again, gaze flashing wildly from the grinning corporal to the grim-faced sergeant with his so determined manner.

Campbell didn't give him a chance. 'All right, Corporal,' he ordered, 'take him round the back.' He hesitated only momentarily, his hand falling to the flap of his pistol holster. 'I'll take care of the Jerry personally.' Almost as if talking to himself, he added in a low voice, 'I've got a lot to pay the bastards back for . . .'

That was how the excited dispatch rider from the New Zealand Division headquarters found them, as he slewed his bike through the slush and the mud. Three Germans with unbuttoned tunics were lying sprawled out on the ground behind the wall in the extravagant postures of those violently killed, while another crouched on his knees wringing his hands in the classic pose of supplication. Above him towered the NCO, twirling the chamber of his big .38 to check if there was still a round there. There was. The

NCO hesitated no longer. He placed the muzzle of the .38 at the base of the weeping SS man's skull. Next moment the back of the man's head erupted in a welter of fig-red thick blood and gleaming white bone. Without even a shriek, the headless body slammed into the mud.

'Oh, my sainted aunt!' the dispatch rider moaned as he pushed up his goggles, as though trying to assure himself that he was seeing correctly. He was. There was no mistaking what had just happened here in this burning township: the little sergeant had just shot a couple of Jerries in cold blood. All of them were sprawled face down in the mud, the back of their heads blown off in a bloody gore through which the shattered skull bone gleamed like polished ivory. The DR swallowed hard and then remembered both his message and the fact that he, the born civvy and devoted coward, was risking his own bloody neck coming up here to the fighting front. He had always left that sort of thing to the hairy-arsed PBI*; they were paid to get themselves bloody killed.

'Sergeant Campbell . . . Campbell 175?' he called out above the rising snap and crackle of the new small arms fight.

Campbell turned slowly, not taking his eyes off the SS man dying at his feet. 'Yes?'

'You're wanted back at HQ . . . PDQ . . . pretty damned quick.'

'What for?' Campbell asked, indicating to the tall Kiwi corporal that he should let the SS kid run for it, taking his message for the SS bastards with him. 'I've got that corporal back there. He knows everything I do.'

Five yards away the corporal grabbed the kid by his long tousled blond hair. 'All right, arse with ears,' he snarled. 'Go on . . . do a bunk.' To emphasize his order, he gave the kid a kick in the rump.

*Poor Bloody Infantry.

The youth stared about him in total confusion. He'd understood. But what were the Tommies letting him go for? Were they going to shoot him in the back when he ran – why should he be saved? He was SS too.

The Kiwi corporal kicked him again, harder this time. The kid waited no longer. He started to hobble away and Campbell relaxed, telling himself he hoped he had done his bit to weaken the German defences up front; the Kiwi PBI needed all the help they could get. He addressed the dispatch rider again, as the latter gunned his engine impatiently. For ahead the German 88mm cannon were already ripping the air apart with a sound like a giant piece of canvas being torn, and plumes of black smoke were now rising in front of the attacking New Zealand infantry. This was a dangerous place for people like himself. 'What's so important?'

'Search me, Sarge . . . all I know is that I've got to bring you back to Monty's headquarters toot sweet.'

That caught Campbell, usually so confident and unflappable, completely by surprise. '*Monty's HQ*, did you say?'

'Yes, Sarge,' he answered, adding a little proudly, 'I'm not local, yer know. I'm Army HQ, Sarge.'

'Strewth!' the Kiwi corporal exclaimed and spat into the mud, as if in wonder. 'I never thought Mrs Higgins' handsome son would see the day when some bloke from Army HQ ever got this far front.' He spat again. 'Wonders never frigging well cease.'

As Campbell 175 was soon to find out this murderous day, 'Mrs Higgins' handsome son' was frigging well right . . .

Major Mackenzie of Special Intelligence looked up as the sergeant that HQ had recommended knocked on the door of his temporary office and entered. Casually, he returned Campbell 175's salute and added, 'Stand at ease . . . Stand easy, that's a good chap.' Mackenzie had long given up the usual army formalities between officers and other ranks.

Indeed, he'd virtually forgotten King's Regulations and nobody in authority was prepared to make him observe them. For he knew and they knew that Mackenzie didn't need the British Army, but the British Army definitely needed him and his expertise – at least till this war with Germany was over.*

He looked down at the notes he had made beforehand, while outside self-important staff officers carrying confidential papers moved back and forth, field telephones buzzed urgently and male clerks, cigarette ends stuck behind left ears, typed away furiously. The new offensive was slowing down again and Monty was 'bellyaching', as the Eighth Army commander always put it. Everyone was on their toes. 'So,' Mackenzie asked after a moment, 'how long have you been Campbell 175, Sergeant?'

Campbell 175 smiled. He hadn't expected the question to be put so directly but he could cope with it, though he hoped this very young major with his sharp eyes and keen face wasn't the usual staff anti-Semite he'd often encountered at headquarters. 'Ever since I volunteered for the shit and shovel brigade – the Pioneer Corps, sir – and the powers that be thought that Heino Hirschmann latterly of Cologne, Germany, wasn't a particularly good name for a British soldier who might be captured by the Germans.'

Mackenzie grinned, too. Campbell 175, who had taken the risky step in 1940 of volunteering for the infantry, was definitely a card – one who had fought bravely for his adopted country. He was shrewd, too. Mackenzie could see that. His very manner revealed that he had that easy continental Jewish ability to sum people up, cut through their pretensions, poses, fake personalities. Why else would

---

*See Leo Kessler: *Murder at Colditz* and *Sirens of Dunkirk* for further details of Major Mackenzie's exploits.

he have approached him in this way with that reference to the 'shit and shovel' brigade for instance?

'All right, Sergeant Campbell,' Mackenzie said, his mind already made up about this former junior partner of *Hirschmann und Sohne* of Cologne. 'Would you like to volunteer to join me?'

Campbell's face grew serious. 'I like my present job, sir. I feel I'm doing something for the boys at the front. I couldn't work here in the staff.'

'You won't have to,' Mackenzie reassured him. 'And between you, me and the gatepost, I have a feeling you won't be doing your present job for long anyway. There are people around here who don't like your methods much.' He looked significantly at the other man.

'I meet brutality with brutality, sir. It works.'

'I'm sure it does, but not everybody likes that kind of brutality.' Mackenzie didn't give Campbell a chance to discuss the matter any further. Indeed, he didn't want to tell Campbell that serious charges had been levelled against him which, if proven, might well land him in the dreaded 'glasshouse' at Aldershot. In a way, as Mackenzie saw it, the job that he would soon offer Campbell could save him from a lengthy jail sentence.

'All right,' he snapped. 'This is the situation. I need someone who can speak fluent Italian. They tell me you do. Good.' He didn't let Campbell agree or disagree, but went on, 'General Montgomery has just given me an important assignment – I've flown out from the UK to tackle it. It concerns our cousins from over the sea.'

Campbell 175 thought he noted a trace of cynicism in the manner that Mackenzie used the popular phrase for their American allies, but he didn't comment. Instead he waited, intrigued now by the hard-looking young major's approach.

'Do you want the transfer and the job, Campbell? I can

tell you, between us, that it might be wiser on your part to say yes *now*.'

Heino Hirschmann, now known as Hector Campbell, was not easily intimidated – he had seen and experienced too much for that in his young life. But the major's manner was compelling. So he said, 'Yessir. I'll transfer.'

'Good,' Mackenzie snapped. 'So this is the set-up. The Yank CIC is baffled.' He looked enquiringly at Campbell to check whether he knew what the initials meant.

Campbell responded with, 'Counter Intelligence Corps, sir?'

'Exactly. They appear to be ex-flatfoots for the most part. They know nothing of Europe and what goes on here. So General Montgomery called me in – and now you, too.'

Campbell was suddenly intrigued. He realized that if the victor of El Alamein, as Monty was now being called, was involved, young Major Mackenzie was up to the neck in something big – very big. He wondered what it was.

Next moment Mackenzie told him and it took Campbell a huge effort of willpower not to whistle aloud when he heard the news.

Mackenzie lowered his voice, as though afraid that someone might be listening at the door and overhear him, passing on information which had now been classified as top secret back in London. 'Four days ago an attempt was made on the life of the Yankee general, George Patton. Patton, though officially still in disgrace, is soon to be returned to London to command an army in the coming invasion.' He paused ever so slightly, and then added, as if he couldn't get the news off his chest quickly enough, 'We are going to find the man – or men – who attempted to murder him.'

Now Campbell gave way to his feelings. Forgetting where he was, he exclaimed in his native German, '*Oh du, Kacke am Christbaum!*'

'You might well say, Campbell. It really is "Great crap on the Christmas tree". Let's get cracking. Time is not on our side . . .'

Two

It was a typical Sicilian street scene in central Palermo where Colonel Codman had arranged to meet Mackenzie and Campbell 175 away from General Patton's HQ in the palazzo.

Barefoot urchins ran back and forth begging from passing GIs, crying '*Sigarettes* . . . *Caramelo* . . . you like sleep with my sister?' and the like, already little adults on the make with their ragged clothes and knowing dark eyes. Street whores slumped in doorways, legs spread, holding their labia apart with their fingers whenever they spotted a soldier who might pay for their services. And here and there, an invariably sharp-eyed Mackenzie spotted runtish little men having their shoes shined or pretending to read a paper, dressed in flamboyant suits and making no attempt to disguise the fact that they were members of the newly returned Mafia. Indeed, they seemed proud of the fact, not really bothering to hide the bulge under their armpits where their concealed guns nestled, although bearing arms was forbidden to Italians.

'The Yanks brought the Mafia back to Sicily and Italy,' Mackenzie explained to Campbell when the latter mentioned the fact, 'supposedly to help them with intelligence. But the Yanks didn't know what they were letting loose here after Musso' – he meant the now deposed Italian dictator, Mussolini – 'had got rid of them. Now the Yanks think they are in charge, but it's those damned little crooks in their cheap flashy suits who are really the bosses here in Sicily.' He indicated one of them who had stopped a couple of white-helmeted American military policemen and was openly handing the big Americans a wad of greasy Italian money. 'As you can see, the Yanks are not slow in learning Mafia ways. No wonder the Mafia control most of the public offices here *and* on the Italian mainland—'

Mackenzie stopped. Codman's jeep was edging its way down the packed noisy street, the Colonel at the wheel adding to the racket by leaning heavily on its horn to clear the begging children out of his way. A moment later it pulled up and Codman got out, red-faced and angry, declaring, 'Those damned wop kids'll be the death of me one day. I'm in a cold sweat worried that I'm gonna run over one of the little buggers.'

Mackenzie gave him a wintry smile and said, saluting the American in a half-hearted way, 'Come on, Colonel. Let's buy you a beer. I think beer's safer than the rotgut hard booze the Eyeties make in their farmhouse stills.'

'You're on, Major. Lead me to it.' Codman nodded to Campbell.' Getting used to the quiet life here in Sicily, Sergeant?'

'Bearing up, sir, thank you,' Campbell replied dutifully and slapped away the hand of one of the barefoot urchins, which furtively tried to undo his holster flap in order, presumably, to steal his revolver and sell it on the black market. '*Porco di Madonna*!' he cursed in his crudest Italian and the tousled-hair kid fled back into the throng.

'*Birra – tutti*,' Campbell ordered, as the three of them seated themselves at a grubby table in one of the roadside bars that lined the piazza.

Out of the corner of his eye Mackenzie noted, as the waiter shuffled away to fetch the weak, fizzy Italian wartime beer, that one of the Mafia types had moved from the shoeshine stand and was now lounging near the door of the bar, puffing in a bored way at his black market US cigarette. He told himself that the Italian was probably just a petty crook, acting out a role expected from him by the cowed populace of the capital city. They thought that the Mafia had its eyes and ears everywhere. He dismissed the matter as Colonel Codman took a grateful drink of the cold beer and said, as the shabby waiter in his worn tailcoat moved back to the counter, 'Now here's the deal, gentlemen. The general states that it was some kind of shooting accident that killed our driver and that it *wasn't* an attempt on his life. Besides,' he grinned momentarily in a tired manner, 'the general maintains that if anyone were to take a potshot at him, he'd know how to defend himself. "You're darn right I would, Codman" – those were his very words.'

Mackenzie nodded, but said nothing. Codman continued, 'Well, I told him that General Eisenhower, the Supreme Commander back in London, England, wanted the matter investigated and that General Montgomery was sending two of his best men to carry out the task. Well,' Codman hesitated, 'he wasn't too happy about that either.'

'What did General Patton say, sir?' Campbell 175 asked a little cheekily.

'Well, let's put it like this, Sergeant. He wasn't very complimentary about your chief.' Codman looked embarrassed. 'In fact he remarked he wondered why . . . er . . . that little limey fart worried about him. After all, everyone knows I had him outclassed by long odds during the campaign in Sicily here.' Codman, the proper Bostonian, actually flushed.

Campbell seemingly enjoyed his discomfiture. He said, 'Your chief, sir, doesn't seem to like General Montgomery. Bit of a card, eh, sir?'

'There are a lot of important people back in the UK who don't like General Montgomery either,' Mackenzie snapped coldly. But although he liked Codman, who was genuinely upset, he told himself that Patton's remarks were typical of the Yanks these days. At the beginning, when they had finally got into the war, they had been very deferential to the British, who had been fighting since '39. Now, because they supplied most of the troops and much of the arms, they felt themselves the top dogs – and they were damned boastful about it, too, in that loud-mouthed Yankee way. He forgot his resentment. 'All right, Colonel, a lot of people in the top brass feel your general is in danger. We're out to find who from. What can you tell us?'

At the door, the little Mafia crook had edged closer, head turned to one side, presumably so that he could hear better, Mackenzie thought.

'Well,' Codman commenced slowly, 'there's the Mafia. As you probably know, Major, we brought some of them over from New York in Operation Underworld?'

Mackenzie nodded while Campbell 175 tensed and started to listen intently.

'It started with those two big-shot hoods Meyer Lansky and Lucky Luciano. When the war started they got in touch with naval intelligence in New York and volunteered to help the men planning the Sicily invasion through their contacts on the island and in southern Italy, primarily in Naples.'

'In return they wanted to be released from jail,' Mackenzie prompted.

'Exactly. But apparently the deal paid off, because they helped us through their old Mafia island network. I mean they had contacts all over Sicily, down to the smallest one-horse wop village, especially up behind us in the mountains. Unfortunately, by the time the Sicilian campaign was over, they'd established themselves back in power here, Italo-Americans who the locals thought had the power of the US Army behind them which, in a way, they had.' He frowned, as if he had suddenly realized the full implications of what he had just said.

31

'But why should the local Mafia feel the need to assassinate your General Patton? He is – *was* – an army commander, disgraced for the time being, but surely one who will move on, leave Sicily, when the call comes for him to take an active command once more.' Major Mackenzie looked at Codman enquiringly.

Again Codman looked embarrassed. Indeed, when the two intelligence men got to know him better, they realized that he was almost permanently embarrassed trying to explain his chief to other people. 'Well, it's like this, Major. The general likes to tell the story of how, as a young man in Texas, he met a panther hunter. The panther hunter was very dark and he apparently had the devil of a job trying to convince his fellow Texans that he wasn't a "Mex", as the chief calls 'em. He told the chief that once a feller had taken him for a Mex and he had to shoot him three times before the other feller was convinced he was white.' Codman shook his head in disbelief while his listeners smiled. 'That's the kind of man the general is. He has his prejudices, a lot of them to be exact. And Sicilians, especially if they belong to the Mafia, are his pet hate at the moment. He is putting intensive pressure on our authorities here to put the Mafia bosses back behind bars, especially if they're from the States. And the Mafia don't like it.'

'All right,' Mackenzie said, 'so the Mafia are a possibility.' He cast a glance at the door out of the corner of his eye. The Mafia watcher had vanished. Mackenzie shrugged. He'd probably got bored with the whispered conversation. 'Who else?'

'I hate to tell you this, Major. But since the slapping incident and the press reports on it, he has been bitterly hated by our own troops. When he addressed the Big Red One – the 1st US Infantry Division to you – before it left the island, he was roundly booed by our own soldiers. That didn't go down well, I can tell you.'

'But would an ordinary squaddie want to bump off a general?' Campbell 175 objected.

'A good point. Under normal circumstances, I don't think so, Sergeant. But the men who fought here and are still here don't live under normal circumstances. Some of them are definitely combat-happy, not altogether right in the head. I mean look over there, for instance.' Codman indicated the other side of the noisy square.

'Oh, very naughty!' Campbell exclaimed when he saw what was going on. In one of the dark doorways, a drunken GI had his flies undone, while one of the down-at-heel whores was busily engaged in rubbing his penis up and down as if it were a piece of useless rubber hose, while all around the barefoot children laughed and giggled, as though it were some kind of adult Punch and Judy show.

'You see, the men don't care. Hell, no one dare carry on like that stateside. The cops'd run them in like lightning.' Codman shook his head in mock wonder, as the soldier started to tremble, his knees seeming to give way beneath his as the urchins applauded. 'The men, especially the frontline guys, are completely out of hand,' the American colonel concluded.

'Possibly,' Mackenzie agreed. 'But that doesn't make them want to kill the commanding general. What about the Germans, for example? They have a vested interest in liquidating General Patton. After all,' Mackenzie chose his words carefully, for he was the only one there who knew that Patton would soon be snatched from his island exile here in Sicily and sent to England to take over an active command, 'sooner or later Patton will be given a new army, perhaps for the invasion of France, and here he proved himself a formidable enemy. I wouldn't put it past the Hun to attempt to get rid of him now.'

Codman sucked his bottom lip thoughtfully. 'Possibly. But at the moment, it looks as if the general will be lucky if he survives to see Christmas. Senator Bailey of South Carolina is currently demanding that the general be court-martialled on account of the slapping incident, and the senate dealing with his promotion to three-star rank has postponed its decision until Patton's conduct is investigated even further.'

Mackenzie dismissed the matter. He drained the rest of his beer impatiently, like a man eager to get to work. 'For the time being we've got enough to go on. We start as soon as we get settled in here.' He pushed back the wooden chair and rose to his feet.

'I've got bachelor officers' quarters arranged for you and the sergeant,' Codman said.

'No thanks, Colonel. Sergeant Campbell here has already fixed us up with something local.'

Campbell grinned knowingly for his own private reasons, but he didn't comment.

'You see, Colonel, for the time being,' Mackenzie went on, 'I don't want to appear to have any connection with the American forces in Sicily especially with General Patton's HQ, which I suspect is being watched. Our cover here will be as representatives of the British War Graves Identification Group. It doesn't exist, of course. I've just made it up.'

Codman looked puzzled and Mackenzie explained. 'We're here to check if all our British dead from the Eighth Army who fell during the Sicilian campaign have been picked up and transferred to the official burying places, which in due course will be turned into regular war cemeteries. You see, Colonel Codman, that will give us enough cover to be able to wander about the place without arousing too much suspicion.'

Codman looked relieved. 'I thought for a while, Major, that you may have gone off us Yanks on account of the general's prejudices. After all, not many folk would like to look after someone who dislikes them so intensely. You

know, "the little limey fart", as he calls your Montgomery
and the like.' He blushed again. 'General Patton is full of
prejudices, I'm afraid.'

'And I'm afraid, Colonel,' Mackenzie responded somewhat harshly, 'the British Empire can no longer afford to be
touchy. We British need all the help we can get these days.'
He sniffed. 'Why else are we working to help save your
General Patton, anglophobe as he might be, from harm?'

Campbell looked up at his new boss. He told himself that
the young major had more to him than just a very smart
pre-war academic who had become a top spy catcher in
recent years. The man was an English patriot, true blood.
He noted the fact for future reference. Then he spoke.
'Perhaps, gentlemen, we ought to get started. If we drop
our gear now, we can have a stroll about and see what we
can see.'

Codman took the hint and rose too. Then he stretched out
his hand as Campbell walked to the door and surveyed the
crowded square as though looking for something definite.
'Good luck, Mackenzie,' Codman said warmly. 'You know
you can rely on me for anything you need. We Yanks are
not all like the general, who's a funny old bird at the best
of times.'

'Thank you, Colonel,' Mackenzie responded with similar
warmth. 'Perhaps you can arrange for me to meet your chief
when he's not in one of his anti-British moods?'

Codman laughed. 'Normally he eats a Limey before
breakfast every weekday. On the seventh day, seeing as
it's Sunday, he relaxes. I'll see if I can get him to see you
on a Sunday, you should be safe then.'

So they parted, with Campbell throwing the American
colonel a tremendous infantryman's salute, his hand trembling visibly as it touched the edge of his forage cap, to
which the American responded with an equally smart salute.
Mackenzie waited till Codman had swung himself into the

jeep next to his driver and said, 'You did him proud with that salute, Sergeant.'

Campbell winked and said, tongue in cheek, 'The Yanks expect that kind of thing from we British chaps, sir. Blind 'em with bullshit, as we used to say in the old mob, the 51st Highland Div.'

'Yes, you British chaps,' Mackenzie commented and then, suddenly very serious, he asked Campbell, 'What did you see?'

'Over there, sir, at three o'clock, next to the church.'

'Got it.'

'The little Eyetie in the fancy suit, tossing coins up like George Raft does in those gangster pictures, sir.'

'I see him.' Mackenzie studied the little Italian in the cheap pinstriped suit, who stared unsmilingly at the crowded scene before him – indeed he looked as if his runtish, swarthy face had never broken into a smile in his entire miserable life – and then asked, 'What about him?'

'I think he might be a big shot, what the Mafia call "*il capo*", the chief. Because the other type reported to him and even those two Yank military policemen gave him a wide berth. Another thing,' Campbell continued.

'Yes?'

'The Eyetie talked to Colonel Codman's driver while he was waiting in the jeep.'

'Perhaps he was trying to beg an American fag. You know what the Eyeties are like?'

Campbell 175 shook his head. 'No, sir, it was the other way about. The Eyetie passed some notes to the driver – and they were not those big greasy bits of paper that the Eyeties use. They were greenbacks.'

'You mean dollars?'

'I do, sir,' Campbell said grimly.

Mackenzie looked thoughtful, staring at the Italian in his flashy suit, flipping his silver coin up and down, as if he

36

hadn't a care in the whole wide world. Finally he spoke. 'Well, Campbell, thanks to you, we know something of significance already.'

Campbell was pleased. 'And what's that sir?'

'That if that runt over there flipping his damn coins à la George Raft is a member of the Mafia as you suppose, Campbell, then those gangsters have someone – the Yank driver – inside General Patton's household.' He stroked his lean jaw thoughtfully. 'I think I ought to have a chat with our general about his internal security sooner rather than later. Come on, let's see this dosshouse where you've quartered us.'

They started to squeeze their way through the noisy throng of the piazza. Behind them the man in the flashy suit stopped flipping his coins. He nodded. A barefoot kid detached himself from the shadows of the nearest doorway. Almost immediately he began to follow the two Englishmen. The strange battle in the shadows had commenced.

Three

Major Mackenzie saw him first from afar, to be exact from the bottom of the hill on which rested his palazzo headquarters. He was standing on the terrace talking to a group of senior officers, with Colonel Codman standing to one side attentively as good aides were supposed to – within summoning distance but yet out of earshot so he could not hear the vital military secrets the great man was undoubtedly revealing to the other top brass.

Patton was taller than Mackenzie had imagined. Most American generals he had met so far in this war had been short and dumpy, looking like civilian business executives who had been forced into flashy, too-tight Bond Street bespoke uniforms. He was different. He looked like a general should. Everything about him – from the lacquered helmet with its three gold stars, to the immaculate riding boots – fitted perfectly, gleamed and glittered, as if his batman had spent hours getting the equipment exactly right so that the general could put it on and start performing as a famous general should. Even when he gestured, standing there on the 18th century terrace of the palazzo – and Patton seemed to gesture a lot – he did so dramatically, using his swagger stick, as though directing imaginary armies into battle.

Despite what he had heard about Patton's anti-British attitude, Major Mackenzie was impressed. The American was totally different from the 'little limey fart' Montgomery, but Patton did have that aura of command about him just like the hated Britisher. Patton, he told himself, would get things done in the field of battle; he was no writing-desk warrior like, say, Eisenhower, the Supreme Commander, who had sent him into exile here in Sicily.

Then Mackenzie dismissed Patton, the warrior, and concentrated on what he should say to the general, for the top brass had now come to attention and were saluting Patton. Codman was edging closer to his chief, obviously trying to catch him before he moved away to some other act of business. Unconsciously Mackenzie tugged at the back of his ill-fitting battledress blouse. Patton, he guessed, would be a stickler for correct dress, even if the soldier was one of those detested limeys.

The other generals were now moving off the terrace to where their automobiles waited for them. Codman had approached Patton, who stood there very erect, holding his swagger stick ever his right shoulder as if it were a rifle. Mackenzie decided it was time to move. Slowly he started to climb the steps. Above him Patton was saying in a rather high-pitched squeaky voice, 'Codman, I've had that wop from the Eyetie Bureau of Antiquities bitching to me again this morning. The wop says that a tortoise shell is missing from the royal suite. Christ on a crutch, Charley, what does the wop take me for – a frigging janitor or some damned thing?'

Inwardly Mackenzie smiled. General Patton was living up to his fearsome liverish reputation. At the British Army's regulation six paces' distance from a senior officer, Mackenzie halted and clicked to attention a little awkwardly, for he thought little of military rituals.

Patton stared at him.

Slowly, his arm rigid, Mackenzie raised his hand to the brim of his cap in salute, the movement followed carefully by a gimlet-eyed Patton. 'General,' he announced, 'my name is Mackenzie. I am a major in a special intelligence unit of the British Army, sir. With your permission, sir, I should like to speak to you, *sir*!'

Slowly, not taking his gaze off Mackenzie for an instant, Patton, too, came to attention. He returned the salute with one of his own, a beautiful, precise, marvellously orchestrated one, before lowering his arm and saying in that strange high-pitched voice of his, 'At ease, Major. Codman here says you have something to tell me about security. Come on inside my little home in the west.' He granted the Englishman a tight wintry smile and walked ahead of the two of them into the ornate baroque palazzo.

Codman and Mackenzie looked at each other. Codman smiled encouragingly and nodded that Mackenzie should go ahead. A little hesitantly, hc did so, wondering exactly how he could convince the general that he was in danger. For Patton looked like a man who had never once been scared in the course of his nearly six decades on this earth.

Patton threw his helmet and swagger cane on to an ornate, fragile-looking table, sat down and crossed his booted legs with a flourish, saying to the two subordinates stood a little awkwardly before him, 'Quite a palace as these things go, eh? They say the chapel has been bombed, but the Eyeties have laid on a catholic priest for my spiritual welfare. Haven't seen him yet. Don't guess I will. I've got my own Holy Joe. Good guy. Episcopalian like me. Don't go much for these Roman types. It ain't normal even for a priest to disdain the pleasures of the flesh, eh?' He grinned challengingly at Mackenzie, displaying his dingy teeth.

Mackenzie got the point. Patton was trying to disconcert him. Suddenly he was a little angry. He had never liked to play games like these. Sharply he said, 'General, we have reason to believe that the local Mafia might be interested in your affairs.'

Patton shrugged. 'So?'

'Well, we feel that their interest might be connected to the attack which killed your previous driver.'

'Have you any hard evidence on this, Major?' Patton's voice was suddenly very harsh.

'The day before yesterday my sergeant saw an Italian, who we believe belongs to the Mafia, hand over money, *American* dollars – which it is illegal for Italians to possess – to another of your drivers. We can only assume that, as the driver didn't sell the Italian anything, cigarettes or the like, the money wasn't for black market goods, but for some kind of service the driver—'

'PFC Jones,' Codman interrupted swiftly.

'Well, some kind of service this Jones, General, must have rendered. My guess is that that service was information about your headquarters here or even about yourself, your habits and so on.'

Mackenzie stopped there. He didn't want to antagonize Patton by going on too long. He guessed that Patton, like all the top brass, had only a limited attention span.

Patton's thin face flushed angrily. 'Goddamit,' he barked, almost to himself, 'I won't have my men taking bribes from those greasers. *No sirree*!' He spun round to Codman. 'Charley, where is this treacherous bastard . . . this Jones guy?'

'He went AWOL, twenty-four hours ago,' Codman answered a little lamely. 'He must have cottoned on to the fact we were after him. When the MP went to his quarters to arrest him, he'd done a bunk.'

Patton flushed even more and Mackenzie could sense his short fuse was going to explode in a second or two. Hastily he stepped in to help an embarrassed Codman, who he had got to like in the couple of days he had known the American colonel. 'I know where this Jones fellow is at the moment, sir,' he said. 'I and my sergeant could have arrested him early this morning. But

41

we're British and he's American. Question of protocol, sir.'

Patton relaxed a little. 'Screw the formalities. You've got my permission to arrest the guy and I want to see him *personally* when you bring him in.' Patton paused and his right hand dropped to his holster. 'I'm touched that you British are so concerned about my welfare. But I can assure you, Major, if anyone attempts to knock off General George Patton, he'll be waiting for him and it won't be the first time I've had the drop on a fellow and shot him before he could do the same to me. Besides,' he added, his voice suddenly quavering, and Mackenzie realized for the first time that, despite his cockiness and loud-mouthed boasting, General Patton was really an old man, 'who would profit from shooting me? What gain would it be for the Krauts, or anybody else for that matter? I'm just a broken-down old fart that's been put out to pasture. No use to anybody any more.' He broke off and at that moment Mackenzie could have sworn he saw the glint of a tear in the general's eyes.

Codman had seen it, too. He knew more than Mackenzie just what an emotional person Patton could be under that rough, tough exterior. He nodded urgently to the Britisher. Mackenzie took the hint. He snapped to attention, replaced his cap and said, 'With your permission, I'll leave now, sir.'

Patton didn't seem to hear. He was clearly preoccupied with his thoughts and they weren't very cheerful. For a moment or two, Mackenzie felt sorry for him. In London they knew that Patton would soon be given a command for the coming invasion in France. But the powers that be were keeping that information from him. Patton was being deliberately led to believe that his days as a combat leader were over. He was being well and truly punished for his 'crime'.

Mackenzie swung the general a salute, did the best

about-turn he had ever done and marched formally down the steps of the palazzo. A moment later he was in the borrowed US jeep, heading for the harbour and what Campbell called 'a third-class knocking shop', where the absent PFC Jones was currently holed up.

A couple of British sailors in their whites were hammering away at each other, oblivious to the crowd, as Mackenzie's jeep arrived at the waterfront. In the harbour more GIs were preparing to be shipped from Sicily to the Italian mainland. Stevedores grunted and heaved. Self-important staff officers hurried back and forth with their clipboards and pencils. All was noise and controlled confusion. But still there were men, soldiers and sailors who could get time off from their duties to stand in line outside the brothels lining the quay, contraceptives in their hands in case the MPs checked, to find some sort of paid sexual pleasure.

They weren't a pleasant sight, Mackenzie told himself as he pushed his way through one line of men to where Campbell was waiting for him, leaning against a crane. Most of the man were drunk and all of them had that eager look about them which said they couldn't get their pants down quick enough to ram themselves into the whores inside. They looked like brutes, but Mackenzie reasoned it was the war that had brutalized them. They were young and most of them probably wouldn't grow much older. Before they died they wanted experience and pleasure, even if it was paid for and given by some raddled Sicilian whore who had probably 'pleasured' half a dozen men already this December morning.

'Well?' he demanded.

'He's still inside,' Campbell answered. 'As far as I could gather there is no back exit. I think he's taken up with one of the tarts. You know, sir, the usual deserter dodge.'

Mackenzie indicated that he did. Smart deserters often found themselves some whore or tart who'd take them in on a long-term basis. She'd supply the rations and the rum, he'd provide the money. That way the deserter would avoid the risk of being picked up on the streets by the military police who were everywhere in big towns these days. 'Any sign of George Raft?'

Campbell shook his head.

'All right,' Mackenzie commanded, 'let's get on with it. And watch it, Sergeant. Keep your eyes peeled – he might be armed.'

Campbell 175 grinned. 'Peeled like the proverbial tinned tomato, sir.'

They passed the two sailors. They had stopped fighting now. Both were panting hard and one was trying to stop the blood flowing from his battered nose. The other who had just punched him was gasping. 'I had to do it, Nobby. I couldn't let yer get away with stealing me bangers, NAAFI bangers at that. What would our messmates in the division say, chum?'

'See what yer mean, Chalky. I never thought of it like that. Just fancied a nice juicy banger and a cup o' Rosie Lee to wash it down, like. Sorry, old mate.'

Mackenzie shook his head in wonder. Every day at sea they stood the chance of being killed, but when they were off duty and safe, what did they do? They went and tried to pulverize each other. There was no way of accounting for hot-blooded young men.

Irma, the proprietor of the knocking shop, opened the door to her establishment personally, for Campbell had already bribed her with a carton of Lucky Strikes. She was short, plump with peroxide blonde hair and huge breasts that seemed about to burst from the confines of her tight red silk blouse. She touched a finger to her blood-red lips in a conspiratorial fashion and whispered '*Prego*'. With exaggerated care she started to lead them up rickety stairs that smelled of garlic, stale tobacco smoke and ancient lechery, her buttocks moving from side to side like well-oiled mechanical parts.

'Christ, sir!' Campbell exclaimed, a little awed at the sight. 'All that meat and no potatoes, eh!'

'Shut up,' Mackenzie hissed and followed the tightly packed, swaying flesh without any further comment.

A little out of breath, Irma paused at the head of the rickety stairs and opened the door. She held a finger to her full, red lips in warning and then went in on tiptoe. She opened the next door to reveal a large room, filled with shabby, worn, plush furniture and yellowing pictures that told immediately what the room was used for. '*Allora*,' she declared proudly, '*il salone.*'

Mackenzie allowed himself a little smile. He could guess what the salon was used for; the pornographic photos on the walls revealed all. Here the girls assembled to meet their clients. But now the salon was empty. Presumably the girls were sleeping off their labours of the previous night.

He guessed right, for Irma said in her fractured English, 'Renate, the cow, she jig-jig.' She made an explicit gesture with her forefinger and the thumb and forefinger of the other hand formed into a circle, in case they didn't understand. 'In the final room.' She inclined her head to the right.

Campbell nodded his understanding and said something rapidly in Italian, pulling out his pistol at the same time.

Irma blanched under her heavy make-up and pressed her plump body against the wall with an audible squeak of her corsets, as if the shooting might start at any moment.

Mackenzie said softly, as though he had the situation perfectly under control, 'You go first, Campbell. When I give the signal, open the door. I go in. If this Jones tries to reach for a weapon, shoot him in the hand or something, but we want him alive. Clear?'

'Clear, sir.'

Mackenzie gave the frightened Irma a swift smile and

then the two of them moved forward, crouched slightly, their bodies already tensed for the searing impact of hot steel striking them, both of them keeping to the outside of the corridor where the floorboards didn't creak so much. They got to the door and halted. Mackenzie listened hard. No sound came from inside the bedroom. Perhaps the two of them were sleeping now. That was all to the good. The best time to arrest a suspect was when he was aroused from a sleep. Normally he'd be too dazed and surprised to react. Mackenzie nodded to Campbell. The latter nodded back. He raised his foot, assuming the bedroom door was locked. He drew a deep breath then smashed his foot down with all his strength, just below the lock. A great crash, a splintering of wood, then Mackenzie was in, pistol held tightly by his side.

Next moment he skidded to a stop. Two people were locked in each other's arms on the rumpled bed, held tight as if in an embrace of violent passion, but this was the passion of death, for it was clearly visible that the woman, who would be Renate, had had her throat cut from ear to ear, and it must have just happened, for her blood was still flowing. As for the man, Jones, he had a knife protruding from the small of his back. It looked as if someone had knifed him first, presumably because he had reached for his pistol which had been hanging from the brass knocker above his head.

'Holy shit!' Campbell exclaimed as he followed Mackenzie into the room. 'What—'

Urgently Mackenzie held up a finger to his lips for silence and with his revolver, gestured to the dirty window. The bottom half was open slightly and in the winter sunshine from outside, Campbell could suddenly see the shadow reflected on the pane of glass. There was someone out there!

Mackenzie nodded significantly, as if to confirm Campbell's own suspicion that whoever was crouching there on the rickety balcony with its rusty railing was the person who had just slit the whore's throat and knifed the American deserter.

Campbell made a dumb show of throwing something at the window and pointing to Mackenzie's pistol. The latter understood immediately. He indicated the whore's purse which lay on the floor among a jumble of underwear she had probably discarded in a drunken haste to please Jones. Campbell got it. He picked up the heavy purse, probably full of virtually worthless Italian lire coins. Next instant he flung it at the window. In that same moment Mackenzie raised his pistol.

The purse slammed against the loose pane. It cracked and the shadowy figure sprang from his hiding place. Mackenzie didn't give him a chance. The woman had been the lowest kind of whore, but she deserved better than having her throat slit. He pulled his trigger and felt the pistol jerk upwards with the force of the explosion. The dark figure shrieked. He raised his hands, flailing the air as though trying to ascend the rungs of an invisible ladder. To no avail. Another scream. Next instant he went over the railing. There was a muted thud as his body slammed into the damp cobbles of the quay below.

Four

'What the Sam Hill are you guys in Sicily doing?' roared the fat American colonel with the bald head at the skinny Italo-American standing opposite him. Outside in the Caserta headquarters of General Clark's Fifth US Army, there was silence now, save for the steady muted tread of the sentries. Most of the HQ personnel were off duty, presumably enjoying themselves in the fleshpots of Naples, which was out of bounds for Clark's fighting troops. Indeed, the fat colonel would have never received the runtish little Italo-American with the shifty dark eyes during normal duty hours. There were too many prying eyes and too much tittle-tattle at the HQ. He didn't want to be seen associating with the new head of Naples' Mafia.

'Listen, Colonel. I'm no *Siciliano*, Colonel, I'm Italian.' He threw out his skinny chest to show he was very proud that he wasn't a Sicilian. 'Those dagos down there are useless. Most of 'em can't fart and chew gum at the same time.' He gave the irate staff officer his crooked, gold-toothed smile. 'Goddam hick foul-ups, the whole bunch of them.'

The staff officer, with the gold sphinx badge of the US Army's Counter-Intelligence Corps on his lapels, wasn't impressed. 'You're all dagos, Gino.' He sneered, but then raised his voice to say, 'Kay, you screwed it up. What are you gonna do about it now?'

The ex-New York gangster considered for a moment, whirling the toothpick he affected from one side of his cruel mouth to the other. Outside an ancient peasant was kicking his mule which had gone down on its forelegs under the weight of the huge pile of brushwood it was carrying. The colonel told himself that the old guy had probably stolen it from the headquarters park. The dagos stole everything; nothing was safe from their thieving dirty paws. 'Well?' he prompted.

'I was thinking I should put in some of my boys instead of using them *Sicilianos*. If they've got "Coins" to start squealing, he'll ruin our Palermo set-up.'

'Kay, how different are *your* dagos from those other dagos down there? I don't want another foul-up, you know, Gino. I know you were in the big time back in New York. But this ain't New York. We're the bosses here.'

'Sure, sure,' the smaller man agreed hastily, pushing out both his hands, palms turned towards the colonel, as if he were physically thrusting him away. 'There'll be no foul-ups now because I'm taking charge of the operation, Colonel.'

The officer wasn't impressed. He sniffed contemptuously, but said nothing. Outside the ancient peasant had given up trying to beat his mule back on to its feet. Instead, with the unthinking cruelty of an impoverished, downtrodden Italian peasant, he had taken out his pocket knife and was digging it hard into the animal's skinny rump. Typical dago, the colonel told himself. They all carried knives just in case. When the chips were down, they didn't fight with their fists like white men did.

'I've got a couple of boys who are trained soldiers,' Gino said slowly, almost as if he were reluctant to give the information. 'They're not Italian . . . They're Russian.'

'*Russians*! . . . *Commies*!' the colonel exploded, looking at Gino as if he had suddenly gone mad. 'What in Sam Hill's name are you doing with Russians?'

'Deserters from the German Army, Colonel. The *tedeschi* took 'em prisoner in Russia. As soon as they got down here, they deserted straight away. I took 'em in because they're good with a gun. But you don't want to know about that, Colonel, do you?'

'You're damned right, I don't. I wish I had never got mixed up in the whole dirty business from the start.' He shook his head. 'But I've got my orders – and orders are orders,' he added mysteriously before asking, 'Kay, how you going to get these commie hitmen of yours across to Sicily? What say a navy patrol checks the fishing boat or whatever you'll use to transport them from the mainland, Gino?'

'It was US Naval Intelligence that brought us here in the first place,' the Italo-American answered easily. 'But we're not going to use a fishing boat this time, Colonel. There's been some trouble with cocaine smuggling—'

'Don't tell me,' the American officer interrupted firmly. 'I don't want to know about that dirty business either.'

Outside there was a rusty squeak of unoiled wheels. The mule was moving again, dragging its cart, also laden with firewood. But the peasant was still digging at its rump with his knife, the blade of which was now red with the poor animal's blood. The colonel told himself the mule would probably never make it to the peasant's hovel.

'Right, you're sending in these Russki hitmen – don't bother me with the details. But this time you're going with them.'

Gino frowned. 'It could be dangerous, Colonel,' he protested.

'Of course it fucking well might. But that's what we're paying you for – and giving you the best protection for your rackets you've ever had in your whole life, don't forget that, Gino.'

The Italo-American's voice took on a whining note. 'Of course, Colonel . . . of course, Colonel. I'll go, don't you worry, sir. I'll see the job is done, sir.'

'It'd better be. And remember this, you've not got a

week to get rid of you-know-who. Things are moving fast at SHAEF HQ*. In the new year there's gonna be changes and we don't want *you-know-who* to be around when they come through. Kay?'

'Kay, Colonel.' The Italo-American would have dearly loved to know who it was that wanted Patton removed. He had to be some big shot, of that he was sure. If he could find out and put the squeeze on him, whoever he was, he was certain the *Organizatione* would be safe in Italy as long as the Americans stayed there. He felt a warm glow spread through his skinny body at the thought. Why, if he could find out who was behind all this, he'd be *capo di capos*, more important than any of those New York bosses who thought they were real big shots. It was then that it came to him. The fat prick would know who the unknown was. Play him along for the sucker he was and the colonel would lead him to the guy who gave him his orders. He feigned a warm smile. 'You can rely on me, Colonel,' he enthused. 'And if you fancy a dame tonight, I've got a real beaut for you. Clean. I have her checked for clap by my own doctor regularly.' He shaped a female contour in the air with his beringed hands. 'What a figure! What a swell pair o' tits. And she can do things to a guy that'll make his eyes pop out. Say, does she do a number, Colonel!' He licked his lips.

The colonel did the same, as if he were suddenly very dry. 'You mean she does . . . *that*?'

'Yessir. She doesn't just *do* it, Colonel, she *enjoys* doing it,' Gino answered enthusiastically. Get the jerk into a honeytrap with Rachele and he'd soon have a hold over him – senior US officers weren't supposed to fraternize with Italian women. Those who did were regarded as a security risk – and the fat pig would soon sing like a yellow canary, once he put the pressure on. 'I tried myself once,

* Supreme Allied Headquarters in London.

51

Colonel, and she did so good that I felt drained down to my toes. Wow!'

Back home the fat colonel had an equally fat wife, who felt that making love with the light on in the privacy of their own bedroom was the height of perversion. Now he was being offered a woman who did things that most guys could only dream of.

Gino could see from the look on the fat pig's face that he was weakening. He pressed home his advantage. 'You don't need to take a staff car, Colonel, in case you think you might be recognized. I gotta taxi outside. An Italian cab. I could take you to her in that. Nobody would see you, Colonel.'

But the little Italo-American was not fated to entrap the colonel just yet. Just as the latter was about to suggest he'd get a raincoat to cover his uniform and take up Gino's offer, the silence of the empty headquarters was shattered by a burst of singing. Outside a bunch of drunken GIs, staggering a little and waving wicker-cased litre bottles of cheap Italian wine, were chortling 'General Clark's Anthem', as it was called at the Caserta HQ.

Stand up and sing the praise of General Clark . . .
Your hearts and voices raise for General Clark . . .
We'll fight, fight, fight with heart and hand . . .
As soldiers true embattled staunch will stand . . .
The Fifth's the best army in the land . . .
FIGHT . . . FIGHT . . . FIGHT!

The fat colonel groaned. Everyone who visited the Fifth Army's entertainment complex at the nearby Palace opera house was given a slip of paper with a copy of the doggerel on it and ordered by a warrant officer to sing it with all their might. The drunks, probably infantrymen on leave from the front, where Clark was hated by his men, were thumbing their noses at the tall, austere and very vain commander of the Fifth Army. The fat colonel didn't mind that. The MPs would take care of the problem soon and the drunks would find themselves back in those dangerous mountains to the north before they knew what had hit them. He was concerned at this moment by the sudden realization that the boss – Clark – would have his ass if he was found stepping out of line with a dangerous dago woman.

The delightful vision of himself nearly naked with a beautiful dago dame gobbling greedily between his spread legs vanished almost as soon as it had come. 'Some other time, Gino. I'll take a rain check on her. But I still want to meet her.' He was very businesslike. 'All right, you know what you have to do. Get those Russkis of yours on the job pronto. This time, don't foul up the job.'

'No, Colonel, you can rely on me.'

'And one other thing.'

'Colonel?'

'If the other guy over there in Sicily hasn't croaked it already, see that he does. Kay?'

'It will be done. But he won't talk if he knows what's good for him. Besides, he's one of us.' Gino said the words proudly.

The colonel didn't hear. His head was already bent over his papers once more. He didn't even say goodbye.

Outside, the drunken GIs were now urinating all over the battered pre-war Italian taxi, or trying to run their bayonets into the great bag of gas on its roof, while the skinny taxi driver ran round and round frantically in an attempt to stop them, getting thoroughly soaked with urine for his efforts.

Gino scowled. What pigs these Americans were, he told himself. He felt his testicles through the hole in his right-hand trouser pocket, through which he could reach the little Biretta twenty-two strapped to the top of his inner thigh. In the manner of the ancient Romans, hand gripping his testicles, he swore his oath of vengeance. One day – one day soon – he'd make the bastards pay for the indignities the Americans had heaped on him and his kind since they had come to Italy as arrogant conquerors. Then he was running through the drunken soldiers, twisting and turning in an attempt to avoid the sprays of urine, crying, 'Come on, guys, give us a break, will ya—' His plea ended in a yell of rage as one of the soldiers, laughing crazily, helmet liner pushed to the back of his cropped head, raised his penis and squirted him from head to toe with hot urine.

Watching from the cover of the ornamental gardens, straining his eyes in the growing darkness, the observer allowed himself a cold smile of satisfaction. The little macaroni was getting what he deserved. The Italian gangster was like all his fellow countrymen, a greasy traitor who'd sell his own mother for a handful of coins.

With a slight groan he raised himself from his hiding place and picked up the bundle of wood stolen from the gardens which were to be his cover if he were stopped by one of the sentries. His artificial leg squeaked. He frowned. Once again he was reminded that he was now a cripple, just half a man. Still, *Wotan* had kept him in its ranks and now he was carrying out an essential mission which might help his embattled comrades one day.

Slowly he started to limp through the growing darkness towards the low wall which surrounded Clark's HQ. The guard caught him by surprise. Later the limping man reasoned that the American had been hiding in the shadows having an illegal smoke which was forbidden while on duty. But now he levelled his tommy-gun at the shabby civilian and growled, 'Hey, what you doing here?'

The observer reacted correctly, prepared as he was for something like this. Appearing to cringe, he whined in Italian, '*Sono veterano de la guerra, Signor Teniente.*' To make his point he slapped his wooden leg with his free hand. As he expected, the leather hinge-strap creaked audibly. '*Povre . . . molto.*'

The guard lowered his tommy-gun. If he hadn't understood the Italian, the gesture had seemingly convinced him that he was dealing with a harmless cripple. 'OK,' he commanded. 'On your way . . . beat it . . . *avanti* . . . and don't let me catch you in these here grounds again, *capisce?*'

'*Si, si . . . grazie, Signor,*' the observer responded hurriedly. He started to hobble away into the darkness, his shoulders bent as if he were weighed down with cares like most Italians were that December. The sentry sniffed and flashed a glance at his watch. Another thirty minutes and his watch would be over. He yawned and was about to turn away when some instinct made him peer through the darkness at the Italian wood collector.

But now the latter was no longer carrying his bundle. He seemed to have gotten rid of it and he was no longer so bent and humble. His shoulders were set back and his head raised as if he had just graduated from West Point or some other military school.

The sentry was puzzled. For a moment his instinct was to challenge the Italian. Then his stomach started to rumble noisily, reminding him it would soon be time for chow and tonight's menu was franks and beans, and he dearly loved franks and beans. He shrugged and dismissed the Italian. What did the dagos matter anyway? They were a crappy beaten nation. What harm could they do? With his stomach rumbling ever more loudly, he started to pace his beat, heading in the general direction of the guardhouse, the Italian now forgotten.

Thirty minutes later, while the young sentry was wolfing down his franks and beans in case those mean bastards of hash slingers called out 'seconds – come and get it!' and he'd be first in line, the observer was squatting in his garret in the blacked-out city, busy with his *Abwehr** radio. At the fastest sending speed he was capable of, just in case the Ami detection vans were trawling the city again, trying to pick up illegal broadcasts, he sent the core of his message: *'Unternehmen Patton lauft hervoragend†* . . . *Unternehmen Patton lauft* . . .' Then switching off the radio, hiding the aerial and sliding the sender down the back of the rumpled cot, which with a single wooden chair and table made up the furniture of the shabby little room, he gazed at himself in the cracked, flyblown mirror. In the manner of lonely hunted men he said to his image, 'Now then, old house, we cripples are also doing our bit for Germany's holy cause.' He raised his glass of grappa and toasted himself in the mirror. *'Sieg Heil!'* he rasped, as they had once done in the good days when they had been young and enthusiastic and every week had seemed to bring a fresh victory for German arms. Then he drained the fiery spirit and next moment, for some reason he couldn't explain, threw the empty glass in despair against the wall . . .

---

* German Secret Service.
† Operation Patton is running splendidly.

Five

'Well, Sergeant?' Mackenzie asked as he stood next to Colonel Codman. 'How's our Italian George Raft getting on?'

Campbell 175 shook his head, his dark face sombre. 'Not so good, sir. Major. Odom—' he looked at Codman.

'The general's personal doctor,' Codman explained swiftly.

'—was kind enough to have a look at the little bastard. He doesn't see much hope for – er – George Raft,' he used the name they had given the man they had first seen in that crowded square flipping his coins like the American movie star.

'I have no interest in keeping the murderous swine alive for longer than five or ten minutes. I just want him to talk, then he can croak in double quick time as far as I'm concerned.' Mackenzie's hard face reflected his bitterness at the fact that their principal lead seemed to be slipping away from them without a clue to who his paymasters were. 'Has he said anything at all?'

Campbell shook his head gloomily. 'A few fragments in Sicilian dialect. I think he was asking for his mother. It's quite common when a man is dying—'

'Let's forgo the comments on life, Sergeant,' Mackenzie snapped.

Campbell wasn't offended. He knew his chief was worried. Patton was being awkward. He was refusing to have

57

bodyguards as Mackenzie had suggested. In his usual boastful manner he had told Codman, 'The guy who can beat
me to draw hasn't been born yet. I don't need bodyguards,
Charley. I'm the best bodyguard for me that I know of.'
And that had been that. Patton had whipped his twin pistols
out lightning-fast, as if he were some movie gunslinger, and
grinned with his dingy teeth. Codman knew there was no
use talking any more. The chief's mind was made up.

'All right,' Mackenzie said as they walked up the gleaming white steps of the Italian hospital which had been
requisitioned along with most of its Italian staff for their
own casualties on mainland Italy. 'Let's take this one step
by step. *One*, an attempt to kill Patton has been made. How
did they know of Patton's movements – the killers, I mean?
Two, probably through that chap Jones. *Three*, Jones had to
be killed before he spilled the beans.' He hesitated, while
Codman showed his pass to the armed sentries in front of
the entrance. Mackenzie had asked him to have them posted
there to keep a guard on the dying George Raft – just in case.
'*Four*, Jones's killer was this George Raft chap and George
Raft belongs to the Mafia, which you Yanks brought back to
Italy and Sicily, Codman. They owe you a debt of gratitude
for that, I suppose. So why would a pro-American bunch of
thugs like the Mafia want to kill an American general, who
one way or another will soon be leaving the island? Tell me
that, please.'

Codman spoke in a lowered voice. 'I can't answer that,
but I can tell you in strictest confidence, Mackenzie, that
General Patton has been completely relieved of his command
now. His Seventh Army is to pass into the command
of General Clark's Fifth Army for the time being. So,'
the American concluded miserably, 'one way or another,
General Patton will be leaving Sicily soon and his run-in
with the local Mafia will be over. Those crooks have nothing
to fear from General Patton.'

Sergeant Campbell waited patiently for the colonel to finish before saying, 'We mustn't forget that these Mafia blokes are just crooks. They owe no allegiance to anyone else themselves. They work for anyone who pays them.' He made the continental gesture of counting notes with his thumb and forefinger. 'Perhaps the Jerries are paying them.' He shrugged expressively. 'Or somebody else.'

'Who?' Codman asked, but Campbell 175 didn't seem to hear the question as they paced down the echoing hospital corridor while white-clad nuns, hands tucked into their voluminous sleeves, glided past like silent white swans. Instead he said, 'So far, gentlemen, we haven't examined the gear,' he indicated a couple of the passing nuns, who also acted as the hospital's nurses, 'they took off old George Raft. It might give us some sort of a clue.'

'It's an idea,' Mackenzie agreed, for he was grasping at straws now. 'Let's hope the nuns didn't burn it.'

'Doubt it, sir,' Campbell 175 said. 'Clothes are strictly rationed here. Besides, your poorer Italians never throw anything away. They're a very thrifty people.'

'Let's hope you're right. Come on. Let's see if we can strike lucky.' The nuns had, as Campbell 175 had surmised, not thrown the dying Italian's bloodstained clothes away. One of them brought in the suit he had been wearing when he was shot, plus his holed shirt – apparently he didn't wear underpants – and placed the clothing on the bench in front of the three of them.

Codman wrinkled his nose at the sight and Mackenzie said, slightly amused, 'Don't worry, Colonel, we won't ask you to search them.' He turned and looked at Campbell 175. The latter gave a little sigh. He said, 'I know, sir . . . I know. I do the searching.'

'I'm afraid you do, Sergeant. Rank hath its privileges, you know. That's why lower ranks get all the dirty jobs. Get to it.'

Campbell grinned and then set to work in a very professional manner. He examined the cheap flashy jacket, searching the pockets thoroughly. Then came the trousers. The few items he found he laid to the far side of the bench. As far as Mackenzie could see they were nothing of importance or any significance. A few nickel coins, a flashy cigarette lighter with a picture of a naked couple on both sides engaged in obscene sex.

Codman, the proper Bostonian, pulled a face. 'Nice taste our killer has!' he exclaimed.

'*Amore*, sir,' Campbell said cheerfully, hauling out a couple of rumpled cigarettes. 'Love is the bread of the poor, sir, that's what the Eyeties say. He stopped short. 'Hello, hello, gentlemen, there's something here in the lining.' His smile vanished immediately.

'What is it?' Mackenzie asked urgently.

'Something in the lining that feels like metal, sir,' Campbell grunted. There was the sound of ripping. A moment later he had what looked like a large nickel coin in his hand, displaying it to the two officers. They peered at it and Mackenzie said, 'That's the fascist insignia, indicating the bundle of sticks which Mussolini's fascists had adopted as a symbol from the ancient Romans.

'Yessir. But do you know what those letters "OVRA" mean?'

Mackenzie shook his head.

'They mean, gentlemen, *Organizzione Vigilanza Repressione Antifascismo.*'

'Organization for the Repression of Anti-Fascism,' Codman translated carefully.

'Yes, Colonel, the fascist secret police under old Musso.' He meant the deposed Italian dictator, Mussolini.

'But what would a Mafioso be doing working for Mussolini when old Musso cracked down on the Mafia in the '20s and '30s?' Mackenzie objected, a puzzled look on his face.

'Of course, I'm not an expert on these affairs, sir,' Campbell answered. 'But as I understand it, sir, when Musso cracked down on the Mafia bosses, sending them into exile, he kept on some of their ordinary followers and enrolled them into his own Gestapo, this OVRA lot, and sent them to other parts of Italy to crack down on his opponents – socialists, communists and the like.' Campbell hesitated for a moment, as if he were uncertain about what he would say next. 'When I got out of Germany in '38, sir, I did it by way of Austria and into the south Tirol . . .'

Mackenzie was about to stop him there, but then thought better of it; the look on Campbell 175's face was too earnest.

'Well,' Campbell went on, 'I got as far as Bolzen where some of the local peasants hid me till I could start the next stage of my escape to Rome. The peasants there were once Austrian and they hated Hitler for not making Musso return the area to Austria when the Führer took it over in '38. But to cut a long story short, I was betrayed. One night the bastards from OVRA surrounded the farm where I was hiding and they started to work me over. They were Sicilian all right, and former Mafia thugs, and they were hand in glove with the Gestapo trying to close up the Jewish escape line into Italy and beyond.' He frowned suddenly. It was as if he was hesitant to go on, and Mackenzie told himself that the young Jewish sergeant had been through worse experiences than he had in his four years in the dangerous business of counter-intelligence.

'Well, first they gave me the old castor oil treatment. It was standard with OVRA. You know, they force the damned stuff down your throat and – excusing my French, gentlemen – you start shitting straight away. Very humiliating and very messy. But they were in a hurry. Once I got my pants down, they whipped out their knives and threatened to castrate me. You know for the Eyeties, with all their sexual pride in their masculinity, that's the ultimate threat. But they didn't want to touch me with their knives when I was such a mess, so they shoved me back in the barn till the bouts of shits were over and promised they'd be back once they'd dealt with the poor peasants who had hidden me.' Campbell shrugged a little helplessly.

'What happened then, Sergeant?' Codman asked in a quiet, almost kindly manner. Obviously he was impressed by the young NCO's terrible story.

'They hadn't taken my belt away – they probably thought that the state I was in I wasn't going to be able to do anything. But I was. With my looped belt I choked the thug who was guarding the door and when he passed out, I battered his face to a pulp with the peasant's shovel. I did it quite coldly just to show the other bastards that the same thing could happen to them. Then I ran for it. I never found out what happened to the peasants who had hidden me – I hope they made it.'

Codman lowered his gaze as if embarrassed, while Mackenzie stared fixedly at the wall, trying to avoid looking at the NCO who had been forced into doing such a terrible thing. Campbell, for his part, looked reflective as though mulling over the events of that night once again. But not for long. He straightened his shoulders and said in his normal voice, 'So, sir, we've got a bit of lead now, haven't we? The little wop was working for his organization here, but at the same time he might well be taking backhanders from the Germans to assassinate General Patton. It would be in *their* interest to get rid of the general.'

'It certainly would,' Codman agreed enthusiastically. 'They know how he went through them here in Sicily, finished off the whole campaign from Gela in the south to Palermo here in the north. In a mere thirty days.'

'With a little help from General Montgomery and his Eighth Army of course,' Mackenzie said with mild cynicism.

'Of course,' Codman agreed immediately. He was a very fair man.

'All right.' Mackenzie's voice hardened. 'As I've said before I don't give a damn if the little bastard lying down there lives or dies. All I want from him is information. Surely, Colonel Codman, that Major Odom of yours, Patton's personal doctor you mentioned, could give the Eyetie a shot of something to pep him up long enough for us to get what we want out of him?'

Codman said, 'I'll ask him. I'm certain it's against professional medical ethics to do so, but Odom is devoted to the general. I think he'll quietly forget his Hippocratic oath if it will help the general. I'll go and telephone him at the palazzo.'

But the American colonel was not fated to call Odom that day. Just as he started to put on his helmet – for although this was not really a war zone, Patton insisted that his staff wore their helmets or liners at all times – a nun came down the corridor with unusual haste, ringing a bell and crying urgently, '*Alarma . . . alarma*!' She glanced through the open door and saw the three of them. In English, she gasped, 'Please . . . help . . . air attack . . . We need everyone to take the wounded to the cellars . . . *Per favore*!' And then she was off again, panting and ringing the bell.

Mackenzie and the other two forgot the dying OVRA man for the moment. Like everyone who served in the Mediterranean area, they knew that both sides routinely bombed hospitals, although they were clearly marked with huge red crosses on their roofs. They couldn't allow bed-ridden men to lie through a bombing attack with no hope of protecting themselves. They had to help.

Six

A thin mist was creeping in from the Straits of Messina. It curled in around Palermo from the harbour like a silent grey cat. It pleased the 'Old Hare', as his younger co-pilots called the bald-headed *Hauptmann der Luftwaffe*. Below him the young hawks lined up in their obsolete Stukas readying themselves for what was to come, eager and desperate for some glory. He smiled cynically to himself as he indicated to the sergeant co-pilot that he should take the Heinkel III in another dog-leg. The 'Old Hare' knew the sergeant was just as eager to survive as he was. Neither of them had any intention of dying for 'Folk, Fatherland and Führer' as the slogan of 1943 had it. Leave that to the young hawks down below.

The pilots were really raw kids, eighteen and nineteen-year-olds rushed through flying school and trained in the simple tactics of obsolete dive-bombers. To the 'Old Hare' they were just flying cannonfodder, fated to die young. They still believed the Stuka to be the invincible weapon of terror – 'the Führer's flying artillery' as it had been in the great days of 1940.

They were so full of piss and vinegar that they didn't seem to realize that the Stuka was at least a hundred kilometres an hour slower than the average Tommy or Ami fighter, and that most Allied anti-aircraft guns could shoot them out of the sky without too much effort. The 'Old Hare' dismissed the young men as they prepared to meet their fate.

Below the young would-be heroes strapped themselves tighter into their cockpits. Their leader gave his teddy bear one last squeeze for luck. He waggled the wings of his Stuka as the signal for the start of the coming attack. He pointed downwards. To left and right the men of his squadron nodded. They'd have to begin now before the mist, rolling in from the Straits, obscured their targets, for the Stuka bombed by aiming itself at the target and then, when it seemed about to dash itself to pieces on the ground below, releasing its bombs and breaking off in a wild curve to the left or right.

'Old Hare' saw the movement of the foolish boy's wings. He readied his own weapon. He touched his throat mike. 'The piss-pansies are about to go, Sergeant. You're in charge. I'll take over the weapon completely.'

'Sir,' the NCO replied. 'Heaven, arse and cloudburst! They're off, sir. Just look at 'em!'

The 'Old Hare' flashed a glance below. Lieutenant Hannes, their leader, his lucky teddy bear mascot now resting on his lap, pushed his stick forward. The Stuka seemed to fall out of the sky. Sirens shrieking in a banshee-like howl, it hurtled downwards towards Palermo, seemingly destined to splatter itself into a thousand pieces. Almost at once the flak took up the challenge. It looked like glowing golf balls, growing ever faster as it rose and rose, the tracer shells headed for the planes.

The lieutenant led a charmed life. To left and right the shells exploded in angry bursts of scarlet flame and smoke. It was as if the lone attacker was flying through a mass of balls of cotton wool. Twice, the observers in the Heinkel thought Hannes had been lost, as his Stuka vanished into the terrible maelstrom of fire. But each time he emerged unscathed, still sinking in that death-defying dive.

Suddenly the whole plane began to tremble. A myriad deadly steel eggs dropped from its blue belly. In the Heinkel the two observers could imagine the scene in the Stuka's cockpit at that moment. The G-force would be terrific. The pilot's face would be flattened under the terrible pressure. For a moment he would black out. Then with all his strength, his arms feeling like lead weights, he would exert the last of his muscle power to jerk the stick back and come out of the tremendous dive before it was too late and he'd hit the ground and disintegrated into a thousand pieces.

Now as his bombs began to explode on Palermo in a rippling wave of red-ringed smoke, the young pilot fought his plane back into the sky, chased by tracer zipping after him like lethal white morse. One by one the others followed, momentarily hovering in the sky like great metal hawks, before screaming downwards.

But now the American flak had got the measure of the obsolete dive-bombers. The gunners concentrated their fire on the steady stream of bombers, circling them with their murderous shelling. The first Stuka was hit. It exploded in mid-air than fell apart in a great ball of angry crimson flames. A second staggered, came out of its dive, thick black smoke trailing from its engine. Desperately the pilot tried to keep it airborne, probably wanting to get the damaged aircraft back across the Straits of Messina. To no avail. Suddenly, startlingly, the engine cut out. The pilot threw back the canopy. The two observers could see him quite clearly, poised there like an expert diver about to make one last spectacular dive. The plane lurched. The pilot was thrown out. They thought they could hear the crack of his parachute opening. But the sound was just in their imagination. A tattered piece of white canopy flew out of the parachute pack on his back. But the chute itself was in ruins. The pilot fell screaming to his death.

Now the slaughter of the Stukas had commenced in earnest. The 'Old Hare' knew it was time to get on with his own mission, now that the defenders of Palermo were fully occupied with the airborne Stuka attack. Repressing his mounting feeling of excitement, he touched his throat mike and said as calmly as he could, 'I'm going to launch now . . . keep her as steady as you can, Sergeant.'

'*Sir!*'

The 'Old Hare' pressed the switch to release their burden. The Heinkel shuddered momentarily and rose twenty metres or so as it was relieved of its extra weight. The 'Old Hare' adjusted swiftly. Peering out he could see the bomb as it swept ahead of the two-engined Heinkel. He nodded his approval. The bomb was doing fine. Often, if the controller wasn't skilled enough, the bomb would take a nosedive immediately after launching and that would be that.

Without orders, the sergeant at the stick brought the Heinkel down slightly. The bomb followed. Over central Palermo as the Stukas still fought their desperate battle with the American defences, the smoke was clearing a little. It was enough, for it enabled him to see their target. But the 'Old Hare' knew that the gunners would soon be spotting him too. Slow as they were, guiding the radio-controlled bomb to its target, they'd be sitting ducks. In the next five minutes they had to be in and out or, as he told himself in his cynical fashion, they'd soon be sitting on a cloud, dressed in white frocks, playing frigging harps. He licked his lips which had suddenly gone very dry. But he kept his nerve. After all, hadn't 'Smiling Albert'* promised him and the sergeant seven days in Rome with all the firewater and *raggazi* they could handle if they pulled this one off. There'd be all the 'tin' they desired, too, but that wasn't important to him. He had a drawerful of medals somewhere or other. He concentrated on the task at hand.

*Smiling Albert, ie Field Marshal Albert Kesselring, German commander-in-chief in Italy, nicknamed thus because he always seemed to be smiling.

The palazzo was clearly outlined now in the circle of fire and smoke created by the Stuka attack. He edged the controls a little to the left. The flying bomb reacted immediately. He pushed the little control stick a shade further to the left. Now he peered through the circular aiming hole; it seemed to 'Old Hare' that he had lined up the bomb with the exact centre of the house where the *Abwehr* spy, that old-legged ex-*Sturmbannführer* of the elite *Wotan* regiment, had reported that the general's living quarters were. Controlling his breathing, not chancing a slip-up at this late stage of the game, he ordered the sergeant at the plane's controls, 'Take her down to near-stalling – *now!*'

The pilot knew exactly what to do. He reduced his speed and, to make sure, he lowered the undercarriage. It was a dangerous manoeuvre but he, too, was an 'old hare' – a veteran; he knew what he was doing. Lowering the undercarriage had the desired effect. The plane's speed decreased even further.

Now the Heinkel was making its last approach. At the controls, the sweating red-faced sergeant fought to keep the plane airborne. At this low speed, one wrong move and he knew she'd fall out of the sky, her twin engines stalled. But he wasn't going to let that happen.

The 'Old Hare' knew he could rely on the sergeant. He concentrated totally on directing the 500 lb bomb on to its target. For some reason he grinned as his thumb tensed above the firing tit. 'Try this one on for collar size,' he said as he commenced the old formula. He broke away the next instant.

Out of a patch of smoke rising in a dark mushroom to starboard, a lone Stuka had appeared. The 'Old Hare' recognized it immediately. It was that of the squadron commander, that young fool with his shitting teddy bear, Lieutenant Hannes. For a moment he forgot the radio-controlled bomb. Why was he coming back to the attack, he asked himself. He had dropped his bomb load. What could he achieve without bombs? Then the 'Old Hare' had it. Lieutenant Hannes was going to attempt a suicide mission. Filled with the same foolish patriotism that the bombastic brown-clad fools of the party back home had drummed into these young idiots since childhood, Hannes was going to dive on the palazzo himself, crash into the Amis' living quarters.

Urgently he touched his throat mike. 'Tiger One to Tiger Two!' he yelled. 'Break to port . . . break to port!'

There was no response.

The 'Old Hare' tried again, his voice raised, even a little panicked. 'Tiger One to Tiger Two . . . *Break to starboard*!'

Again there was no response. For a moment the 'Old Hare' almost lost control of himself. The situation was totally confused. To starboard the remaining Stukas were literally being slaughtered. In a sky that was a bloody network of smoke and flame – and sudden death – Stuka after Stuka was being hit. On all sides they were screaming into their dives of death, trailing scarlet torches behind them, parachutes blossoming in white bursts as the young pilots tried to escape the inevitable. Now the 'Old Hare' himself would be on a collision course with Hannes if he attempted to continue guiding the radio-bomb on to the palazzo. There was no more room for manouvre back through the dying Stukas. What in the three devils' name was he to do?

The decision was made for the veteran. Hannes was falling out of the sky, his face set in a grimace of death. The green needle of his altimeter shot down alarmingly . . . *300 metres . . . 250 . . . 200 . . . !*

Frantically the 'Old Hare' tried to launch his bomb before it was too late. He hadn't reckoned on this situation with his fellow veteran, the sergeant pilot. He flung the plane off the prescribed course, eyes wild with horror as the Stuka came howling out of the sky at him. In absolute panic he flung up his arm as if to blot out the horrifying sight of impending collision. To no avail. The black shape seemed to fill the whole world. In the same instant that the 'Old Hare' launched his bomb uselessly, the Stuka smashed into the slow-moving Heinkel with a great hollow boom and rending of tortured metal. The two planes locked together inextricably and went hurtling down to the wounded city below. Harmlessly, the flying bomb splashed into the sea and lay there impotent. The raid was over . . .

'Well, bugger this for a tale of soldiers!' Mackenzie snorted and puffed out his cheeks in exasperation. There was no doubt about it. The little Mafia-OVRA agent they had called George Raft was dead. There wasn't a mark on him as he lay there on the floor with the other dead. But he and they were just as dead as the once-owners of the pieces of limbs that hung from the shattered trees outside like pieces of obscene red human fruit. According to the Italian surgeon who had examined George Raft, his lungs had burst just like the others' had with the blast that swept through that part of the requisitioned hospital.

Mackenzie looked down at him for one last time and then said, as if talking to himself, 'Well, we'll get no more out of that little bastard.' He nodded silently to Campbell 175. Together they clambered over the still smoking rubble of the shattered ward into the coolness of the afternoon, grateful for the fresh air after the fetid, bloody smell of the dead.

Somewhere a wounded American was singing crazily, 'Over there, over there . . . Give a cheer for the Yanks are coming . . . have a care . . . over there . . .' Mackenzie told himself that perhaps the young GI had gone crazy with too much morphine. Not that it mattered. The whole bloody world had gone crazy. He paused and, taking out the silver cigarette case presented to him by Mr Churchill, he took out a Capstan. As an afterthought he offered the case to the young Jewish sergeant.

The latter shook his head. 'Give up smoking, sir. They say it's bad for your health.' He gave a hollow cynical laugh and Mackenzie understood. Once he might have reprimanded an NCO for making a remark like that. Not now. How old and cynical he felt now, his youth totally vanished after four years of brutal war.

He watched as the Italian orderlies started to load a group of dead nuns on to a mule-drawn cart. They treated them with respect, not throwing them up like logs of wood as soldiers would have done, but passing them carefully, seeing that their habits were pulled down so as not to reveal their bare legs. The ones who had been stripped naked by the blast they covered almost reverently with mattress covers or blankets or anything else they could. But they could do little with the one who lay in pieces on a door, like offal placed there by a butcher to be taken away and processed in some meat plant.

Campbell looked up at his chief's face in the growing darkness. 'Do you think we'd better be going back to HQ, sir?' he suggested softly. 'There's nothing much more we can do here, is there? I think this is a job for the Graves Commission, not us.'

Mackenzie nodded silently. He didn't notice the solicitude in his sergeant's voice.

Slowly they walked to the jeep where Codman was waiting for them, shrouded in gloom like they were, smoking moodily. Beside him the driver gunned his engine as if he couldn't get away quickly enough from this dreadful scene of murder and mayhem. Mackenzie asked, 'Everything all right with your general, Colonel?'

'Yes. Thanks.' Codman took the cigarette out of his mouth, as the driver engaged first gear. 'Funny thing though.'

'What?'

'That glider bomb I told you about over the phone.'

'Yes?'

'It was plotted so that it would hit the palazzo and, my guess is, strike the general's quarters in particular.'

Mackenzie shook off his dazed, introverted mood. Suddenly he was alert, apprehensive even. 'So, what makes you worried, Colonel?'

'Not worried, *puzzled*, Mackenzie. You see,' he concluded as the driver started to move away, steering in and out of the box-like ambulances carrying the wounded to the port to be shipped across the Straits of Messina to more specialist hospitals on the mainland. 'If that little wop, you know, George Raft, was working for the Krauts and intended to kill the general, why go to all the trouble of a Stuka attack feint while that Heinkel directed a glider bomb at our HQ? I mean, it was buttering the cake unnecessarily don't you think, Mackenzie?'

But Mackenzie, as smart as he was, had no answer to that overwhelming question.

SECTION TWO

Heaven Help a Sailor on a Night Like This

One

The one-legged *Abwehr* man limped along the quay, noting the mist beginning to form over the Straits of Messina once again. He was glad. It would afford the cover they needed to cross the five kilometres to Sicily. Not that he lacked confidence in the English deserter who would be in charge of the craft taking them across. He was a very skilled seaman, but then, he told himself, the English were an island race. They knew a lot about the sea and ships.

The two Russians were waiting for him at the end of the quay. They were dressed in shabby Italian clothes, provided for them by Gino. But they could hardly be taken for typical Italians. They were both quite tall and possessed that cornsilk hair and bright blue eyes peculiar to *Volksdeutsche** – 'booty Germans', as they had called them when *Reichsführer* Heinrich Himmler had first begun to recruit them into the SS back in '42.

As casually as he could, though his heart was beating like a trip hammer with nervous excitement, he approached them. The two young men appeared to take no notice of him until he pulled out a limp stub of a cigarette and asked in Italian for a light.

Yuri, the bigger of the two, pulled out his precious lighter and lit it, holding it close to the *Abwehr* man's face, as though afraid that the damp mist coming from the sea might

*Ethnic Germans from Eastern Europe.

put the flame out. 'We sail in an hour,' he whispered in German. 'The macaroni has arranged everything.'

'Good,' the *Abwehr* man whispered back. 'I have been instructed to tell you not to take any unnecessary risks. Do the job as planned and remember, we must compromise the Amis.' He shrugged. 'If Patton gets killed, so be it. But the main thing is to compromise the Amis.'

Stefan, the Ukrainian smiled. 'Don't worry, we'll do our utmost. But I wish we could go back to simple soldiering at the front. This life is too complicated for me.'

The agent said, 'How do you think I feel with this tin leg o' mine? I'd rather be back with the old heap, killing Ivans in the East. No matter. Do your best. *Hals and Beinbruch, Jungs.*'*

'*Danke Sturmbannführer,*' they whispered in unison and for a moment the *Abwehr* man was afraid they were going to click to attention. But they didn't and he touched his hand to cap in thanks for the light and limped away. Out of the corner of his eye he spotted the shore patrol: a petty officer accompanied by two Italian police, wearing British battledress but with the dark black cap and flaming grenade badge of the *Carbiniere*. He felt a cold finger of fear trace its way down to the small of his back. He prayed they weren't heading for Yuri and Stefan. He knew they had the correct documents provided by Gino, but their poor Italian would give them away.

He stopped at a derrick and reached inside his ragged pants for the pistol he kept taped to the inside of his right thigh. If it came to the worst, he'd have to use it on either the bulls or the two booty Germans. He daren't risk the plot coming out.

But the *Abwehr* agent was not going to be forced to use his biretta this particular afternoon, for in the very instant the

---

*Break your arm and leg, literally, ie 'happy landings'.

petty officer indicated the two blond Italians, a raucous voice broke the muted silence of the mist-bound quay singing:

> *'They say there's a troop ship bound for the land we*
>   *love and adore . . .*
> *Bless 'em all . . .*
> *The long and the short and the tall . . .*
> *You'll get no promotion this side of the ocean,*
> *So cheer up me lads . . .*
> *Fuck 'em all!'*

The petty officer turned sharply as if something red-hot had been applied to his rear end, his mouth open ready to shout a harsh command. But the command died in his throat. For staggering towards him, his arm round the plump waist of one of the dockside whores, who for some reason was wearing frilly red silk knickers on her head, was a small man dressed in the uniform of his own service, the Royal Navy. And this particular member of the 'Senior Service' was no less than a chief petty officer, his skinny chest heavy with rows of medal ribbons.

He raised his hand, as if to stop the two *carbinieri*, and came to a position of attention. Behind them the two gunmen slipped away as the shore patrol officer said, suddenly all sweetness and light, 'If you don't mind, Chiefie, I'd like to ask you to keep it down to a quiet roar.'

The 'chiefie' staggered to a stop and looked at the policeman whose face looked as if it had been hacked out of granite and said thickly, 'Whatyer say, sonny?'

The other man flushed red. No one had called him 'sonny' since he had run away, a kid in short pants, from his elementary school to become a boy seaman. But he repeated his request.

The chief petty officer took a swig out of the bottle of grappa he was carrying, squeezed the whore's nearest breast and said, 'Bloody lash-up when an old chiefie – who's old enough to be your father, sonny – is told off for a bit of singing . . . Old farts like me don't get much fun in life, yer knows. A drop o' booze and a bit of the other and that's yet lot, sonny.' He squeezed the whore's breast again. She giggled, displaying a mouthful of gold teeth. The chief petty officer laughed at the sight and winked knowingly at the red-faced shore patrolman. 'Sonny, when she goes down on yer, you might come away richer than when you started with them choppers. Look at all that frigging gold!'

The patrolman had met types like the drunken chiefie before – matelots who had served in the navy since Nelson's time. There was no use reasoning with them when they'd had a skinful. The best way was to humour them. 'I'll see yer and – er – your lady friend to your ship, Chiefie.'

The other man creased his wrinkled, tanned face into an attempted wink. 'I know your kind, yer randy bugger. Get me to me bunk and before yer can say Jack Robinson, yer'll have yer filthy paw up my tart's knickers.' He took another swig at the grappa and started to chortle, 'And the mate at the wheel had a bloody good feel at the girl I left behind me . . . Where was the engine driver when the boiler bust? They found his bollocks and the same to you—' But suddenly he ran out of breath. He gasped, 'All right, sonny, I'll go quietly. Take me to my ship. Home, James, and don't spare the horses.'

The shore patrolman gave a sigh of relief.

Five minutes later they had found the drunken chief petty officer's ship – a rusty old landing barge which stank of bilge water, diesel and stale food. Not that its appearance or stink seemed to worry the wizened little CPO, for he gave the whore an elaborate bow, bussed her wetly on her berouged face and announced, 'I bid you farewell, my lovely. I shall now board my noble ship—' He stumbled and would have fallen if the shore patrolman hadn't caught him in the nick of time. But this near catastrophe didn't put him off his stroke. Looking up as the two Italian *carbinieri* saluted, while the fat whore waved her handkerchief sadly, tears streaming down her cheeks, he called to the shore patrolman, 'Tell yer one thing, sonny, my fiancée ain't a true blonde. You can tell that from this angle.' Guffawing crazily, he staggered to the wheelhouse and clambered inside unsteadily. He winked to himself and said, 'Bertie, old lad, the rozzers'd have to get up earlier in the morning to catch you out.' His voice was that of a perfectly sober – well almost – lively cockney, who had been fooling sundry masters-at-arms, shore patrols and 'number ones' in twenty-odd years in the Old Royal.

Bertie Reynolds – 'born in the sound of Bow Bells, and don't you forget it, matey, a real cockney *I* am' – had decided to join the 'Free English', as he called them, the day after he'd taken part in the Salerno landing and had his little altercation with the burly beachmaster from the Royal Engineers with his 'frigging poundnotish' voice and high-handed manner. He had just picked up a load of wounded and had been about to cast off with his 'crew' – a boy seaman, an ancient three-striper and the black boy who came from one of the colonies – when the beachmaster had bellowed at him through his loudhailer, 'Stop that craft – *there!*'

He had pretended not to hear. 'Cast off aft,' he had ordered, the motors running already, drowning the moans of the wounded, stretched out in their bloody field dressings in the well of the craft.

'Stop or I fire!' the beachmaster had bellowed and with his free hand had pulled out his revolver. 'Do you hear – *stop or I'll fire.*'

He'd stopped and the fat, red-faced major had come panting through the tangled debris of the assault landing to look up at him and yell, 'Unload those wounded – at once!'

He hadn't believed his own ears. 'Unload the wounded, sir?' he'd gasped.

'You heard me, petty officer. Get those wounded off at once. *I'm* in command here. You obey my orders without question or it'll be the worse for you.'

'But—'

'No bloody buts!' the officer had cut him off brutally. 'Get those wounded off. We've got a priority-one shipment for Allied HQ. It's got to go *now*, is that understood?'

He had glared at the old sailor and, if he had had a weapon in his hand at that moment, Bertie Reynolds would have shot the big, red-faced officer dead on the spot and damn the consequences. But he hadn't. He and the others had set about unloading the wounded, some of them bearing a red tag tied to their bloody battledress like a luggage label to indicate they were grave cases, not daring to look them in the eyes as the wounded realized they were going back to the beach, which was once again coming in for heavy German shelling. As helpless as they were, they knew they wouldn't have a chance if the enemy zeroed in on their particular stretch of Salerno beach.

Two days later, after he had delivered his 'priority-one' cargo – which later turned out to be a collection of documents captured from a German paymaster's office – he had joined the 'Free English'.

In the hills around the fleshpots of Naples, there were many like him: hardbitten deserters who would stop at nothing in their desperate attempts not to be returned to the front line, where they'd most probably die that winter, when riflemen barely survived a month in combat.

Mostly they were private soldiers who had disguised themselves as officers by making the necessary badges of rank out of cardboard, then headed for the remote villages of the Apennines to call for the local mayor and demand the surrender of all arms. Once that was done, they took over. They ruled by terror, became tyrants, taking anything they wanted, including the local women. Now and again they ventured to the outskirts of Naples, where they set up roadblocks and ambushed Allied supply lorries, especially those driven by unarmed, and usually very frightened, US Army soldiers.

For a week or so Bertie had joined some of them. But their brutality and drunken rapacity had soon sickened him. It was then he had met Gino, the little Italo-American, who had told him about a racket that would take him away from the terror and murder of the mountains. He, Bertie, was to become the skipper of a bona fide (well, almost bona fide) Royal Navy landing barge, which was plying its official duties across the Straits of Messina from Reggio to Palermo.

Naturally, Bertie knew he was working for the Mafia, but he had jumped at the opportunity to return to the cleaner – if somewhat crooked – life of the open sea. Like himself, his 'crew' – a deserter from the Royal Marines, known as 'Bull', as in bullshit, and Harry, a toothless ex-naval gunner who was always complaining that 'you can't make a matelot who ain't got no teeth fight – no teeth, no fight' – were not bad men. They were just old hands who had been in the war too long. Their courage had slowly oozed away, or they had been sickened by the constant killing, or they had simply given up: men who had been tried too long, seen too many of their shipmates killed and couldn't take any more.

But on their rusty old tub, just the three of them, going about their seafaring duties as if in peacetime, well-oiled with cheap dago red and knowing there'd always be a plump Eyetie pigeon in one of the ports' knocking shops with whom they could dance a 'mattress polka', they were relatively happy men. They felt they weren't harming anybody by ferrying the Mafia's black market goods back and forth. Above all, they had left the savagery and cruelty of the mountains behind.

Of course Bertie Reynolds, old chiefie that he was, knew it wouldn't last for ever. Gino kept them well supplied with false papers and the like, but one day there'd be some officious bastard like that red-faced beachmaster with his cut glass voice who would discover their papers were fake and then it would be curtains. Yet, like he said to his crew as they sat in their smelly little cabin of an evening, drinking the cheap strong Italian vino straight from the bottle, 'Sup up, lads. There's not much pleasure in this world for yer average matelot. When the chop comes, well . . .' and he'd shrug his skinny shoulders. 'Let's make a frigging handsome corpse . . .'

Two

M ackenzie had not wanted to make love to the Italian girl. He hadn't thought it right. She was a servant in the run-down Palermo hotel in which he and Campbell were staying, and he guessed the humble Italians who staffed it felt they had to do anything and everything to please their new masters – even spreading their legs for them, whether they liked it or not. Besides, his Italian was poor and the relationship had become purely sexual with little charm.

It had started, as always, between the conquered and the conquerors. He had offered her some coffee and a carton of cigarettes that he had obtained in the American PX. Whether she could use them herself or sell them on the black market – coffee and cigarettes were the real currency of Sicily – it didn't matter. It had begun the relationship. Adriana – that was her name – had accepted them with a sweet girlish smile and a slight curtsey in the peasant fashion, though Mackenzie later discovered she was anything but a peasant.

Later that evening when she had seen Campbell drive away to eat supper at the American HQ (food at the hotel was just pasta with tomato sauce and whatever the two Britons could provide from their own rations) Adriana had knocked so quietly on the door of his room that he had not heard her for a little while.

She had stood at his door in a kind of embarrassed silence while he had stared at her pretty young face with those great liquid Italian eyes, knowing why she was there and what she was offering, and at the same time not wanting to know. The silence seemed to go on for ever, while Mackenzie's brain raced electrically.

He was no longer the sensitive, clever young academic he had been at the beginning of the war – that now seemed like another age. Calm and controlled as he seemed on the surface, the new Major Mackenzie was now a man in conflict with himself. Something inside of him raged all the time so that if he allowed it to do so, a bitter hatred, a cutting cynicism could burst out with icy, murderous force. He knew it was the strain of the war and the things he had been forced to do in the line of duty.

As perceptive and intelligent as he was, he realized the pretty little maid was offering herself to him in this strange, silent manner, not even attempting to look seductive. Now what was he to do? With the whores and good-time girls he usually frequented back at base in London, it was easy. Get them drunk, offer them hard cash if necessary, and then get down to business. But with this Adriana it was different.

Suddenly she broke her silence. In a soft, hesitant voice, she asked, 'Have you a need of anything, sir?' She lowered her gaze momentarily and in the poor light from a shaded bulb in the corridor outside, it seemed she had blushed slightly.

Then he had made up his mind. 'Yes,' he said quickly, not wanting time to reconsider. '*You* . . . please . . .'

Ten minutes later, armed with a bottle of grappa, he was in her tiny little room at the top of the run-down hotel. Below, the lights of the city were slowly being extinguished as the blackout descended and the searchlights flickered on, parting the darkening sky with their icy fingers, looking for the intruders who came to kill.

In the light of the naked eletric bulb, hung with old, used flypapers, the only furniture a bed and two hard-backed chairs, and with the cloyingly sentimental holy pictures of the Virgin holding a glaring pink heart, they sat opposite each other, sipping the fiery spirit from two chipped glasses she had brought up the from the basement kitchen far below.

Outside, Palermo grew progressively more silent. There was a curfew enforced on both civilians and military. From the port brothel district there was still some noise as drunken sailors and whores carried out their sordid business. But in the end the noise from that direction died away, too; the Italian police would now have cleared the bordellos. Now the only sound was the slow grind of US military jeeps patrolling the streets and the heavy tread of the foot patrols doing the same.

Sitting there, not saying much, they might as well have been the last people alive in the world. Perhaps they were wondering what they were doing there as the little room grew more chilly; it was that old wartime feeling that Mackenzie, a lonely man (his job required him to be) had experienced before. It felt like something would just happen here and that would be it. Nothing would come from it. If one survived the conflict it would be with a mental snapshot of a time and a place, complete in itself. In this case it would be of a crummy hotel, complete with hasty sex, in Sicily, December 20th, 1943. But for once, Mackenzie would be wrong . . .

For a while, as they talked softly – and by now a little drunkenly, thanks to the grappa – he tried to visualize her naked with her shabby skirts and blouse removed: a nubile body, with abundant dark pubic hair at the base of a rounded stomach, her breasts large for her size. But it didn't work. He couldn't get aroused enough to just take her in his arms, throw her on the bed and take her just like that. He felt the desire of course, but somehow he couldn't take that final step. There was something about her that was just too innocent and shy.

At about one o'clock, the bottle now finished as they chatted in whispers for fear of being overheard, Adriana started to cry, softly and without any apparent cause. Suddenly his heart, as hard as it had become, went out to her. He forgot his inhibitions, the anger that seemed to rage inside him all the time these days. Gently he took her in his arms. Perhaps it was the drink, but he found himself whispering stupid, infantile things, words he had almost forgotten, comforting her, kissing her tenderly, and then it happened . . .

Dawn came once more. Outside the port began to wake up again. There was the rattle of the early morning tram taking the workers to their factories, the noise of the carts coming in from the countryside bringing what vegetables were available for the city's market. The night was over. Mackenzie blinked his eyes. His head ached a little with all the grappa he had drunk, but despite that he felt happy – happier than he had been for a long time.

He eased his arm from beneath Adriana. She was still asleep, a silly girlish smile on her lips. He looked down at her with pleasure. Dressed, she had seemed a mere girl. Naked as she was now, she had the body of a woman. Her breasts were full and her nipples were big and dun-coloured. Her pubic hair, too, was jet black and bushy. And during the night she had displayed the sexual passion of a mature woman, clinging to him with something akin to fury as he had pumped himself in and out of her, gasping frantically, as if she were running a race. Once she screamed out so loud that he had had to clamp his hand over her mouth to stop her waking up the whole place. In the quieter phases of their love-making she had talked to him in tight little whispers, sometimes in Italian and then in a mixture of broken English and Italian, relating the story of her humble life as a country girl who had been sent to

Palermo to earn money to help support her typically large peasant family.

Her mother had cautioned her to be chaste, to never give in to a man till he married her. If she lost her virginity before marriage, no man would ever want to marry her; she would have to become a *putana*. '*Figlia mia*,' her mother had declared, just before the ramshackle bus had arrived to take Adriana and her old carpet bag filled with her bits and pieces to Palermo. 'You will swear on the picture of the Holy Mary that you will remain pure.' She had sworn that she would do so, with her hand held on the same cheap picture that now decorated her little room.

But it hadn't worked out that way. Adriana had paused, as if she hesitated to tell him what had happened to her a month after she had arrived in Palermo. Finally she had told him, as far away a church clock chimed two and the city was finally shrouded in a deathly silence so that her whispered account was clearly audible.

Once again it had been the curse of Sicily – the recently returned Mafia. The first of their agents, recruited by New York Naval Intelligence with the help of the two gangsters Meyer Lansky and 'Lucky' Luciano, had slipped into Sicily just before the Allied invasion of the island in July 1943. He had taken up his clandestine residence in the very hotel in which she had worked. According to Adriana, he had been a scar-faced show-off who spoke Italian with an American accent and made much of his time in the 'organization' as he called it, running crooked deals all over the States. His real name was Gi-Gi Cicconi, but he let it be known that back in the States his friends had called him Giggles.

At that point she had tip-toed across to the place where she kept the picture of the Virgin Mary, on which she had sworn the oath to her mother not to lose her virginity until she was married. From underneath she took out a photo. It was of a group of men photographed with their arms around each other's shoulders, squinting into the sun and looking very pleased with themselves. Some of them were in US uniform with badges of rank and pistols strapped to their waists. Two in the middle, however, wore civilian suits of the same flashy type worn by the late 'George Raft'.

Mackenzie had wondered where all this was leading, but he didn't stop her. What she was to relate was obviously very important to her. 'That is Gino,' she pointed to the smaller of the two in civvies. 'He was the *capo*. He came here to Palermo one – two days – after the liberation. This,' and in the dim light cast by the single bulb, Mackenzie had observed how her face had suddenly contorted with hatred, 'is Giggles.' She held up the photo so he could see it better and for a moment he thought her hatred was so strong that she might spit on it.

She didn't and he was able to see a dark-skinned man with a great hook of a nose, his eyes furtive with a mixture of menace and peasant cunning, despite the smile he was presenting to the unknown photographer. It was a face, Mackenzie told himself, remembering a phrase from his Yorkshire youth, that only a mother could love.

Abruptly her look of naked hatred was replaced by one of sorrow. She let the photograph drop on the bed and with her beautiful dark eyes brimming suddenly with tears, she said simply, 'He fuck me.'

For an instant Mackenzie could not quite understand. Was she telling him that this old bald-headed crook with his shifty gaze had been her lover, or what? Then he realized. The man had taken her by force. 'He raped you!' he snorted.

'Yes,' she answered simply, but her voice was thick with emotion. 'In his room below here. He push me on the bed and do it to me. I did not want. He said I must. If not, my parents – they hurt.'

Her language was crude, broken and without the emotion that Mackenzie knew from his own experience normally accompanied such a confession. Yet he felt her shock, and a moment later he was overcome by a sense of outrage at what this 'Giggles' had done to her. 'But you were barely sixteen,' he said. 'Did you not go to the police?'

She shook her head. 'What use? They were important people. I am a girl from country . . . a nobody . . . Besides, they come back here since. This Giggles and his friend, the *capo* Gino. They come across the water from Reggio.' She shrugged a little helplessly. 'If I talk,' she made a gesture of pulling the trigger of a pistol, 'they kill me.'

The news had shaken Mackenzie. He was about to ask for more information, but suddenly her lips had quivered as if she might break down completely and begin sobbing broken-heartedly. Her voice thick with emotion, she whispered, 'Now you not like me, eh?'

His hard heart went out to her. Instinctively he reached for her naked body and pressed her to his own. 'Of course I like you, Adriana. You are a good girl. It was not your fault. It was that swine Giggles' fault.' He squeezed her hard. 'I like you a lot.' The warmth of her nubile body had done it once more. He felt himself being aroused. Passion surged powerfully through his lean hard body. She felt him grow harder and pressed her plump stomach against his hardness. Her breath came in short sharp gasps. His did the same. His questions were forgotten. Like two blind people they groped for each other and then Giggles, the Mafia, the whole world was forgotten.

She spread her legs. He levered himself up on to his elbows. He slid himself into her hot, wet nothingness. She gasped and swung her legs around his back, trapping him inside her. It was all perfectly natural, nothing was planned. Nothing was said. Thus they commenced their wild, exciting, dramatic ride into oblivion. His muscles became like rocks as he clenched her to him. Her heart beat crazily. Her breath came in great hectic gasps as they rode each other to climax, the world outside forgotten, as if it had never even existed. And then with a great explosion of breath it was over and they lay gasping wildly, hot and soaked with sweat, like two stranded, dying fish.

That had been the last time and for a few minutes Mackenzie had found happiness and hoped she had too. But now as dawn came and she whispered she must go to the *toiletto*, he remembered her almost tearful account of Giggles who had raped her and his *capo* Gino. Abruptly he was aware again of his duty and the reason why he and Campbell had come to this Mafia-cursed island in the first place. Swiftly he slipped out of bed and took the picture of the smiling 'liberators' from beneath that of the Virgin. He put on his vest and placed the stolen picture beneath it. By the time she had returned, still naked and sleepy-eyed, he was pulling on his khaki slacks and battledress blouse.

Three

'What d'ye make o' them Eyeties, Chiefie?' Bull asked, busy as usual with his button stick, polishing his globe and laurel cap badge of which he was so proud, despite his desertion from the Royal Marines.

The old petty officer at the controls of the old landing craft that was wallowing its way across the Straits of Messina sniffed. 'Not much,' he answered after some consideration, helped by a swig of the cheap red wine placed at his feet.

Outside the little bridge the mist was coming in fast once more. It would, he thought, give them some protection from the nosey Yanks who were always patrolling this stretch of water, almost as if they expected the German Navy to come attacking in force at any moment. He sniffed, hawked and spat neatly out of the bridge on to the rusty deck below. 'Yanks – I've shat 'em,' he growled, apropos of nothing.

'I mean to say,' Bull breathed hard on the badge and, holding it with the button stick, gave it another polish. 'They don't look much like dagos to me for one thing. Yeller hair and blue eyes – and big with it. They could even be marines. Fine pair of shoulders on both o' them.'

'Marines – I've shat them for breakfast as well,' the old chiefie commented scornfully and added, 'But yer right, Bull. They don't look like Eyeties and I've noticed that when they're by themsens, they don't talk the Eyetie lingo.'

'You been spying on 'em, eh?' Bull said and, holding his beautifully polished badge as if it were a thing of tremendous beauty so that he didn't leave any finger marks on its shiny surface, gently slipped it back in place on his immaculate beret.

'Course I have. I want to know what's going on on my ship. I mean, Gino's paying us to get 'em across, but that little wop bugger'd stab yer in the back as soon as he'd looked at yer. Don't trust him. All them Eyeties are the same – treacherous buggers.'

'Aye, yer right there, Chiefie,' Bull agreed, taking off his web belt prior to polishing its already gleaming brasses.

Outside the mist was thickening even further. Now in the distance they could hear the mournful cry of ship foghorns like frightened children calling for a lost mother. Chiefie blinked his eyes to clear them so that he could see better; he decided he'd stop hitting the dago red, as Gino called the local wine in pseudo-American. He didn't want a collision with two strange, alleged Eyeties aboard and a cargo of stolen petrol nicked from some US Army storage depot by the Mafia and intended for sale on the Sicilian black market. Besides, hidden in the panel of the little bridge there was a soft package wrapped in oilskin which he was supposed to deliver personally to a spot in the main market in Palermo and somehow the little chief petty officer suspected it contained dope. He bit his bottom lip at the thought. Dope was serious. If the Yanks nabbed him with that in his possession, he'd be for the yardarm.

He dismissed the worrying thought and concentrated on his steering. By now they had to be half way across the Straits and it was usually about here that US Navy patrol boats concentrated their activities – and being Yanks their crews tended to shoot first and ask questions later. 'Shit-scared and sodding itchy trigger fingers,' he muttered to himself, while next to him a happy Bull started applying metal polish to the brass, using his button stick expertly to prevent any of the polish falling on his newly blancoed webbing. Simple things please simple minds, Chiefie told himself and then, speaking out loud, cried, 'Arry, get the kettle on, mate. I think it's about time to splice the main brace. Give them so-called Eyeties some hot rum as well. The poor sods'll be freezing their goolies off out there.'

Harry, the toothless ex-three-striper, mumbled something. But as always, without his teeth he was unintelligible. It didn't matter what he said anyway, old Chiefie thought. But the drink of hot rum and tea which he was about to take to their two passengers would give him a chance to have another look at them. For just like their boss, Gino, he didn't trust them. And both of them had suspicious bulges under their right shoulders, which Chiefie knew from his recent experience of these Mafia types indicated they were carrying illegal weapons; for all Italians, whether they were working for the Allies in an official capacity or not, were forbidden to possess firearms.

Time passed leadenly. At the speed his old tub was making, wallowing in water like a dying whale, Chiefie knew it would be at least another half hour before they reached the northern coast of Sicily and started looking for the lonely beach to the south of Palermo where they usually landed their illegal cargoes, which would then be taken away by mule by the downtrodden peasants who were bullied into working for them by the Mafia. Normally it was as easy as falling off a log for an old salt like Bertie Reynolds. But the fog could make it tricky, especially as the lonely bay that was their objective was protected by a rocky outcrop, difficult enough to see at any time, but now made treacherous by the wet mist.

It was about then that Chiefie was overcome by a sudden feeling of apprehension. He didn't know why, but it came out of the blue, an uneasy sensation that something – something unpleasant – was going to happen. Like all old salts he had always known he had a kind of sixth sense for that kind of thing. Sailors had to if they were going to survive, fighting not only the two-legged enemy but also that much more frightening one – the sea. He shivered suddenly, and without really knowing why, snapped at Bull, 'Put that frigging housework down, will yer. Get to frigging port and see if you can see summat.'

Surprised by old Chiefie's tone, Bull didn't protest. Carefully he placed his precious polished belt down and carried out the order. Standing at the steel side of the ugly craft wallowing in the wavelets that had suddenly appeared, indicating to the sea-going marine that they were getting close to the shore, he turned his head into the faint wind and strained his ears.

'Well?' Chiefie demanded from the bridge in a hoarse whisper.

'Nowt, Chiefie . . . Hang on. Sound of engines.'

'One of them Eyetie fishing boats?' the older man asked hopefully.

'Nah, more powerful . . . Coming in this direction and all.'

'Bollocks,' Chiefie cursed. 'That's frigging well torn it!'

Bull strained his ears harder. He realized that the powerful engine running at slow speed was no Italian fishing boat powered by a clapped-out engine with third-rate diesel oil. This was navy, probably US Navy. 'Chiefie,' he called hoarsely. 'I think yer ought to play yer act. I think the Yanks is coming.'

He was right. For floating over the distance separating the two craft, a coarse voice could now be heard singing in a definite American accent:

> *Momma's on the bottom . . .*
> *Poppa's on the top . . .*
> *Baby's in the crib, shouting,*
> *'Give it to her, Pop' . . .*

The unknown's voice rose as he sung the chorus to the domestic idyll:

> *'Who the fuck are we? . . .*
> *We're the raiders of the night.*
> *We'd rather fuck than fight!'*

'How true . . . How fucking true!' Chiefie intoned somewhat mournfully. Then as the engine noise got ever closer and he could hear the muted commands from its bridge, he prepared to put on his old act. He hadn't reckoned, however, with the two blond 'Eyeties' hidden among the drums of black market fuel.

Now out of the damp mist the rakish prow of an American torpedo boat came into view. By looking hard, Chiefie could just make out the figures standing on deck, dressed in long black slickers, a couple of them carrying boathooks. He knew what he was in for if he didn't fool the Yanks at the outset – a full search – and that would be disastrous. He started into his usual act, well rehearsed for such unfortunate occasions. 'Hello there, skipper. Having trouble? Can I give yer a hand? Ha, ha!'

'Cut out the wisecracks!' came the harsh reply through the swirling mist, and Chiefie could just make out a white-capped shape standing on the little bridge. He guessed the speaker was probably the skipper. Usually these small torpedo boats were manned by a handful of ratings and at the most two junior officers.

'Just trying to be helpful,' he said under his breath as the question he had been expecting from the American came.

'What ship are you?'

'His Majesty's Landing Craft, Number 206,' he replied truthfully enough, though he didn't point out that the Landing Craft Number 206 didn't really belong to His Majesty, King-Emperor, George VI, but to the American wop Gino,

95

stolen two months or so before from one of the US Navy repair yards at Naples. 'Proceeding on her lawful occasions, sir,' he added, using an old salt's nautical expression.

'I said cut out the wisecracks,' the American answered back, his voice as harsh as before. 'What's the nature of your cargo, Petty Officer . . . and where are you bound for?'

'POL supplies for RN Depot 6 in Palermo, sir,' he replied, mixing half-truths in with his lies, his voice as friendly and as cheerful as ever. Behind him Bull, who had been through this kind of interchange before, now started to play his own little part in the proceedings.

'Chief Petty Officer. like to report, Chiefie, having a bit of trouble with the POL. Some of them petrol drums seem to be leaking, like.'

Chiefie waited. Usually in such cases, any ship close to a landing barge carrying such dangerous cargo as leaking petrol drums, would sheer off smartish. But this night Bertie Reynolds was to be disappointed. The harsh voice snapped, 'Heave to, Petty Officer. I'm sending a boarding party over to inspect. See that all naked flames – cigarettes and the like – are extinguished immediately. Is that understood?'

'Yessir. Perfectly, sir,' he replied as if he was talking to the captain of the *Warspite*, his old ship before he had been transferred to the landing barge flotilla. 'Immediately, sir.' Under his breath he cursed, 'You bloody hard-nosed bugger. Why can't yer sheer off and let a poor bloke earn a modest crust?' To Bull he said, 'All right, marine, cut along and stop the engines.'

'Aye aye, Chief Petty Officer,' Bull sang out loudly as a good marine should, but a suddenly worried Chiefie could hear the note of anxiety in his voice. He knew why. The two of them had survived a couple of these inspections by the bloody officious Yanks, but then they had been carrying no human cargo. Now they had the two yellow-haired 'Eyeties' stowed away among the drums of petrol. How were they going to explain those two sods away if the Yanks discovered them? Chiefie suddenly felt scared.

The landing barge's engines stopped. She wallowed in the water. Across the way, the motor torpedo boat approached at dead slow speed through the mist, a rating standing on her fore deck ready, Chiefie guessed, with his grappling hook to pull the two craft close together and link them with a hawser so that the inspectors could come on board.

Wildly Chiefie cast around for some way to avoid the search. There was no way he could escape by making a run for it once the Yanks stopped their engines. The mist wasn't thick enough for him to hide and the rocky coast of Sicily was still half a mile or so away. He might have been able to play hide-and-seek with the Yanks there, but he couldn't reach it before the Yanks opened fire with the 37mm quick-firer on the fore deck. 'Christ Almighty, Bertie!' he cursed to himself. 'Get yer frigging thinking cap and do summat!'

But it was the two blond Eyeties who *did* do something – and it was something very drastic that would alter the course of the little naval deserter's life, short as it was to be.

In the same instant that the rating on the fore deck of the US torpedo boat brought his grappling iron down with a clang on the rusty steel side of Chiefie's landing craft, there was the sharp crack of a large calibre pistol. It was like the sound of a twig being snapped underfoot in a bone-dry forest.

On the bridge of the American craft, the officer in the white cap suddenly clawed the air frantically, as though trying to climb the rungs of an invisible ladder. Next instant he pitched forward on his face, dead before he hit the deck.

It was almost as if it were the signal for the fusillade of fire that now broke out as the two big men began squeezing off well-aimed shots from their heavy automatics at the completely surprised Americans.

'Cor ferk a duck!' the little petty officer moaned. 'That's gorn and bleeding well torn it!'

It had. Another rating went down. The heavy .45 bullet smashed into his face making it look as if someone had thrown a handful of strawberry jam on to it. Another rating raced across the deck in an attempt to escape, to no avail. Yuri snapped off a quick burst. The man was hit in mid-stride. Next moment he went over the side, screaming piteously.

'*Avanti,*' Stefan, the Ukrainian, yelled at Bertie. When the latter didn't react immediately he cried, '*Davoi . . . Boshe moi . . . Davoi!*'

Although Chiefie didn't understand the language, he got the meaning all right. He opened the throttle and kicked in the engine. The old barge trembled and then she started moving while on the other craft a brave American ran at a crouch for the quick-firer, ready to turn it on the escaping landing craft. Yuri didn't give him a chance. He fired without seeming to aim. The gunner screamed. Next moment he slumped across the breech of the quick-firer.

'Frig this for a game o' soldiers,' Bertie cursed to himself as he willed the landing craft to gather speed and escape to the rocky coast, before the other officer from the American torpedo boat could whip off a radio message to Reggio or Palermo summoning help. He was in serious trouble and he knew it, more serious than anything before. The US Navy and the Mafia might well be working hand in glove, but the Yanks would never tolerate their men being slaughtered in cold blood by their erstwhile allies. Everyone connected with this merciless bloody shootout would be for the chop if the Yanks caught them and he, Mrs Reynolds' handsome son, didn't intend to be one of them. But how? How was he going to swing it?

For the moment, as the landing craft started to draw away slowly and return fire broke out on the deck of the torpedo boat as somebody opened up with a tommy-gun, sending spurts of lethal fire towards the escaping barge, he had to dismiss the problem and concentrate on the job at hand.

Yuri helped. In the garish light from the burning bridge, which one of the bullets had somehow or other set alight, Chiefie caught a glimpse of the blond Eyetie pulling something from the inside of his shabby jacket. Later he told himself it was what his old dad, a veteran of the trenches in the Great War, had called a 'potato masher', a German stick grenade. But at that moment, carried away by the nervous tension of it all, Chiefie took little notice of what was an unusual weapon for a Mafia thug.

Now Yuri raised it above his head, ignoring the slugs from the Yanks that were cutting the air all around him. With a grunt, exerting all his strength, he flung it at the drifting, blazing torpedo boat. He had not misjudged his aim. The grenade landed with a rattle at the base of the stricken ship's radio mast. Next moment it exploded in a ball of angry purple flame. The radio mast was struck. It crumbled immediately and came tumbling down in a crazy mass of crackling blue flames and sparks. Yuri had put the torpedo boat's radio out of action for the time being. Slowly the landing barge began to disappear into the mist once more, leaving behind the helpless, sinking torpedo boat. At the helm, Chiefie took off his battered cap and wiped the sweat from his wizened, wrinkled face. He breathed a sigh of relief. For the time being they were safe, but for how bloody long he could only guess.

Four

It was a fine December morning. Indeed, the weather was so good and warm that the two Englishmen had decided to have their meagre breakfast of ersatz Italian coffee, bitter and sugarless, plus jammed slices of American white bread, the envy of their Italian neighbours, outside in the little pavement cafe attached to their run-down hotel.

In the square, handfuls of off-duty British sailors and American blacks wandered around aimlessly, pretending not to know what they were supposed to do, though in effect they were looking for women. They were bothered by ragged barefoot children, shouting for sweets and 'cigarettes for Papa', and in some cases offering their alleged sisters with 'you like clean girl, sailor? . . . All pink and clean inside.' And all the while the Italians who had business in the square – stallholders, peasant women selling potatoes and the like – watched in interest, as if this foreign invasion was there merely as a new spectacle to lighten their humdrum routine life.

The little maid, Adriana, came out again with another plateful of the fine white bread and jam, which extracted gasps of awe from the Italian spectators. Before Campbell 175 could take a piece Mackenzie said, 'Tell her, Sergeant, the rest is for her. The poor girl looks half starved.'

Campbell flashed his chief a look but did as he was ordered, whereupon Adriana blushed, gave a little half-curtsey and went away, but not before Campbell had caught the swift glance she had given Mackenzie. Inside his head a mildly cynical voice said, 'So that's the way of it, eh?' Then he got down to business. 'Sir, I've got the details of the two Eyeties on the photo you – er – apprehended,' he said, thinking that 'apprehended' was a better word than 'nicked'. 'The Giggles chap was a small-town brothel owner in various parts of the USA before he ended up in New York where he worked the rackets on the docks. According to my information, the Mafia there always worked closely with the local labour unions to control – *and milk* – the unfortunate dock-workers. Anyway, that is academic.'

'Why?' Mackenzie asked, noting that Adriana was looking at him from the open door of the shabby hotel.

'Because he's dead,' Campbell answered. 'Apparently he was drunk in Naples when he bumped into a US tank. The tank won the engagement. I don't think the US Army sent flowers. Besides there wasn't much left of him when they scraped him up off the road – not enough for a proper funeral.' He smiled cynically at his boss.

But Mackenzie was in no mood for humour, cynical or otherwise. He was too puzzled by the Patton case and his new relationship with the teenage maid. He wondered if he had done the wrong thing by going to bed with her. When this Patton business was over, he'd have to move on, and what would happen to her then? Would she become that *putana*, the whore, that her mother feared she would?

'This other one, Gino, is still alive, and he is much more important,' Campbell was saying. 'If anyone is involved in this nasty business here in Palermo, it's him. He's got his dirty finger into all sorts of dirty pies.' He smiled proudly at his knowledge of idiomatic English. Mackenzie desisted from telling that he had got that particular English saying slightly wrong. Instead he commanded, 'All right, Campbell, please fill me in.'

'Sir.' Campbell was very businesslike now. 'Gino Vittorio

– he's very proud of the name 'Victory' – was actually born in the States, in the Bronx. As a kid he was sent to a reformatory in upper New York State for constant petty theft. "Nickel and dime stuff", as my US informant described it. At all events he must have impressed the local Mafia, because when he finally got out he was taken into the brotherhood and made his bones when he was barely twenty years of age.'

'Bones?' Mackenzie queried.

'Killed someone,' Campbell replied. 'Then he did something foolish. He was apprehended running girls for prostitution from state to state. In America that is a federal offence. Anyway, back in '38 the FBI caught up with him and he got fifteen to twenty years in Sing-Sing. That's where Lucky Luciano and the other Mafioso, Lansky, caught up with him. Lansky got Mr *Victory*,' he emphasized the name cynically, 'out on parole, as the Yanks call it, providing he volunteered to come to Sicily before the invasion of the island last July and get the information the Yanks needed for their landings. He did so using the old Italo-American contacts of the Mafia and was suitably rewarded. He was sent to Naples to help the AMG government there.'*

'Fine bedfellows the Yanks have,' Mackenzie commented. Opposite at the door Adriana was eating one of the jam sandwiches, making her enjoyment of the fine white bread quite clear for his sake, it seemed. He smiled slightly, and again Campbell noted the interchange and wondered if his boss knew what he was getting himself into. Relationships with Italian girls were not as easy as with the ladies of the night they had been used to in London; you couldn't just pay them off and that was that. The *raggazi* tended to cling.

'So what's this Gino Vittorio's position now?' Mackenzie asked. 'Does he fit into our scheme of things?'

*American Military Government of the local civilians.

Campbell didn't answer immediately. His clever Jewish face took on a puzzled look. Finally he said, 'He does in a way, sir, and then in another he doesn't. In fact, I must admit, sir, the whole bloody situation – if you'll forgive my French – is confused. At all events I know it puzzles me. As you've said yourself, if these Mafia types are working for the Jerries, why did the Germans waste a squadron of Stukas in order to cover for their glider bomb attack on Patton's palazzo? It doesn't make sense. You know the German expression *"doppelgemoppelt".*'

Mackenzie, the pre-war D Phil of Hamburg University, who spoke fluent German, nodded his agreement. 'Exactly, why the double? A waste of effort. Unless—'

'Unless what, sir?' Campbell snapped eagerly.

'Unless there is some other element involved, one we have not considered so far.' His words came slowly, as if he were thinking aloud. 'We have the Mafia . . . We have the Hun. Both parties have reasons for wanting to get rid of Patton. But who haven't we considered? Who else might have suffcient interest to want to assassinate him?' He shrugged. 'Can you think of anyone, Campbell?'

The latter shook his head. 'No, sir. I can't think it would be one of his soldiers, unless he were some sort of madman.'

For a while there was a lull in their discussion, as if it were too much of a strain to pursue the matter further. Instead they sat in the winter sunshine, seemingly enjoying the simple pleasure of being alive on a fine December morning like this while only a handful of miles away, desperate young men were fighting and dying in the mountains. The young maid had disappeared now, her bread eaten, to carry out her morning duties, singing happily to herself as she made the beds, as if she, too, hadn't a care in the world.

It was like this that Colonel Codman found them, as his driver honked his way through the usual crowd in the piazza, shouting at the Italian peddlars and beggars and prostitutes

103

to 'get out of the frigging way', but without too much success. Not that Codman seemed in a particular hurry. He paused at the door of the hotel to order more coffee for them and then sauntered to where Mackenzie and Campbell were seated, apparently deep in thought. 'Penny for 'em,' he said cheerfully.

'Don't think they'd be worth that much,' Mackenzie answered, a little startled, attempting to rise to his feet until Codman said, 'Let's forget military courtesy, Mackenzie. I come to bring you glad tidings of a civilian nature.' He beamed down at them as the waiter in the shabby black tailcoat brought their ersatz coffee.

'What's that?'

Codman waited till the waiter had poured the acorn coffee and departed. 'The general's going to give a party. At least, his staff is going to give one for him.'

The news caught the two Englishmen off guard. 'A party!' Mackenzie exclaimed. 'Why now?'

'You mean when the boss is in the doghouse?' Codman said quite cheerfully. 'Because in five days' time it's going to be Christmas.'

Campbell cleared his throat and said carefully, 'Your general doesn't quite look the sort of man who'd be too keen to celebrate Christmas, the feast of sweetness and light sort of thing.'

Codman laughed. 'I know what you mean, Sergeant. No, we of his staff thought it might be good for his image if the press were invited to see him with a lot of Italian kids and local worthies, instead of doing his usual martial bit with the helmet and the pistols, you know.'

Mackenzie kept his thoughts to himself. He knew Montgomery was a bit of a showman too, but American generals went the whole hog with their tough names – 'Wild Bill', 'Iron Mike', 'Blood and Guts' sort of thing – and those tough guy poses of theirs. It didn't go down too well with English sensibilities. Then suddenly he had a thought which at first alarmed him, yet as he considered it a little more, intrigued him as well. Just as Codman was saying that they were going to have a snake charmer for the kids and that the general had sworn that 'if there's any monkey business about draping a frigging cobra around *his* neck, he'd shoot the snake charmer first and the frigging snake next', he interrupted. 'Colonel, if this is going to be a local sort of thing, you'll have to publicize it, won't you?'

'Sure,' Codman said easily. 'That's really the object of the exercise. Good local publicity and good copy for the American readers back home. Our hope is that it'll help to remove some of the stigma attached to the general in the States ever since that foolish slapping incident in the hospital. Why do you ask?'

But Mackenzie responded to this question with another of his own. 'So there's going to be a lot of people without any really effective identification coming to the palazzo, eh?'

'Yes, we can do little about that. But of course, Mackenzie, we shall keep our eyes open, if that's worrying you. But the palazzo's a big old rambling place and we've only got one company of infantry left for guard and ceremonial troops. The front in Italy is crying out for riflemen and General Clark, the commander of the US Fifth Army who is, between you and me, no friend of General Patton, is being pretty strict on the number of troops we can keep under command. But we'll do our best.'

Mackenzie nodded. 'I'm sure you will,' he said. Campbell, watching the two of them, realized that his boss was in no way concerned whether the single guard company could effectively look after Patton. He was planning to set a trap. Once the locals knew that the general was going to be at the palazzo for this Christmas party and that some of them were invited, the assassins – whoever they really were – would see this as an ideal opportunity to carry out their dirty work. In essence, Mackenzie was attempting to force the killers out into the open – and nab them. He smiled to himself. The boss was a cunning old bugger.

But if that was Mackenzie's plan he mentioned nothing of it to Colonel Codman. Instead he pulled out the photo he had stolen from Adriana's room (though Campbell didn't know where he had found it) and changed the subject. 'We suspect the two men in the middle of this snap are somehow connected with the first attempt on the general's life. This one,' he pointed at Giggles, 'is out of the picture now, in a manner of speaking. He had an unfortunate accident with an American tank.'

Codman looked a little puzzled but said nothing.

'This one,' he pointed to Vittorio, 'is still in the picture.'

'You mean "Joe Victory", as he likes to call himself.' Codman recognized the Mafia man immediately. 'A big shot in Naples now.'

'You know him?'

'Everybody who's anybody in Naples does. Sure I know his background, Major, and that he's a former Mafia hood, but he did help us a lot here in Sicily and since then he seems to be keeping his nose clean.'

Mackenzie wasn't impressed. Bluntly he said, 'Colonel Codman, I want that thug, nose clean or not, to be arrested this very day. Can it be done?' The American looked perplexed. 'Well, yeah,' he answered hesitantly. 'It can be done, but Joe Victory's got plenty of pull at General Clark's HQ at Caserta. He's got friends. I don't know whether they'd let him be arrested—'

Mackenzie cut him short with a curt, 'Colonel Codman, if we want to save General Patton from an assassin's bullet, I think you'd better ensure that this Joe Victory is arrested as soon as possible.' He rose to his feet, ignoring a red-faced Codman. 'Come on, Campbell, we've got work to do.' With that, not waiting to see if Campbell was following, he was pushing his way through the mob to their own jeep. Behind them Codman pushed his cap to the back of his balding head and whispered to no one in particular, 'The limeys! No wonder the general hates their frigging arrogant guts . . .'

Five

'*Stand by*!' Bertie Reynolds hissed urgently to his crew. The ugly landing craft was coming in at a rush now. Ahead they could hear the waves roaring as they smashed into the unseen rocks.

'What yer gonna do, Chiefie?' Bull asked, holding on tightly as the unwieldly barge heaved to and fro, battered by the wild white water.

'Just get fit to go over the side and bloody run for it,' the wizened old petty officer whispered. 'And get the lead outa yer arse, or yer might have lead in yer frigging back. Now hold on.'

Now the sound of the waves and the noise of the water slammed into the rocks, followed an instant later by the deep-throated roar of the withdrawing sea and slither of gravel that drowned even the throb of the barge's engines. Chiefie knew they were very near. Indeed now he could see the stark outline of the rocks with a black smudge of land beyond. He tensed. It was going to be now or never, for he had guessed what their fate was to be once he had beached the landing barge. The three of them had seen too much. The two killers who had slaughtered the crew of the Yank torpedo boat were not going to let them survive to become witnesses against them. Already the two of them were talking urgently to one another in a language that was not Italian, and they had still not put their pistols away. He knew why. They were about to be selected as the killers'

108

next victims and, as he had told himself when they had commenced their run-in to that isolated Sicilian beach, 'Mrs Reynolds' handsome son ain't about to turn up his toes and snuff it – just yet.'

Now the unwieldy, blunt-nosed landing barge was becoming very difficult to handle. He prayed that he could keep her on an even keel till he reached the shallows. His escape plan depended upon it. For if he lowered the ramp forward as was customary with such craft and they attempted to go out that way, the two killers would gun them down before they even reached the end of the steel ramp.

He groaned and exerted every muscle. The craft was damnably hard to hold on an even course. But he had to! Behind, Bull and Harry tensed and Bertie sensed that behind them the two killers were doing the same, ducking at intervals as the spray came flying over the steel sides of the old landing craft.

To his immediate front a large rock loomed up. Wild white water poured down its sides. He thanked God that it did. He wouldn't have seen it if it had not been for that water. The muscles of his skinny shoulders burning as if they were being prodded by red-hot pokers, he wrenched the wheel to port. There was a rending, tearing sound. Metal on stone. For a moment his heart seemed to stop beating. He babbled a swift prayer. It was the first since he had run away from grade five of his elementary school to join the old Royal. This dawn God was with him. The screeching of tortured metal ceased and they were past the big rock. The time had come to put his desperate plan into action.

He squinted his eyes against the wind and the icy flying spray. Now he could make out the rest of the obstacles in his way. There were rocks very close to port and the rip tide was running in that direction. He'd need all his skill and strength to avoid them. But he knew if he didn't, he'd be a dead man in the next five or ten minutes. This was it.

He took a deep breath and then he was running in at twice the old tub's normal speed and veering dangerously to port. The waves smashed against her sides. She reeled under the impact. Urgently they grabbed again for holds, all save the drenched little Chiefie. His hands were like stone, gripping the wheel, knowing it would be fatal now if he let the maelstrom wrench the controls from him.

They came closer and closer to the rocks that loomed larger and larger. Now they seemed to fill the whole world. All was rock and the banshee howl of the wind. It was nature against man, the danger posed by the two killers forgotten in this duel of man against the elements.

Chiefie blinked over and over again. The water struck him in icy douches. But he daren't attempt to wipe his face. He must hold on till the very last. There was an ugly grinding of the keel. They were in shallow water.

He acted. They were virtually past the rocks to port. With the last of his strength, his shoulder muscles on fire with the terrible strain of holding the craft true to course, he swung her round. He braced himself for the shock, as did the other two of his crew, who knew what he was attempting to do. The landing craft quivered like something alive. Here and there, rivets popped with the tremendous strain. Next moment the craft hit the shingled beach with a rending crash, her bottom torn out so that she heeled broadside on, throwing the two surprised killers to the deck.

'*Run for it, lads!*' Chiefie yelled at the top of his voice above the roar of the waves. Without waiting to see if they were carrying out his command, he flung himself over the upturned side. He hit the ground hard. For a moment, he crouched there, winded, the icy waves splashing all over him.

'*Stoi!*' The cry in Russian – though he didn't know it was Russian – alerted him to the danger. He clambered to his feet. Scarlet flame stabbed the darkness. A slug howled off the upturned keel a couple of feet away.

'Frig this for a tale of soldiers,' he cursed to no one in particular. He started to stumble up the steep beach. He slipped on the wet gravel. It was good that he did so. Another bullet missed him by inches. He stumbled on.

Now the Russians were scrambling over the side of the stranded landing barge too. They were not going to let the eyewitnesses to their crimes get away. The two of them were younger and a lot fitter than their intended victims. They got poor toothless Harry first. Less agile than Bull and Chiefie, he had attempted to go to ground behind the rocks till the Russians had chased after the other two. It was a fatal decision.

Yuri heard him chattering with the cold in his shelter, as the spray was blown over him time and time again. He grinned evilly to himself. Stooping, he grabbed a handful of wet sand. Expertly he lobbed it to the far side of the rock behind which the old sailor was hiding. Harry reacted as Yuri had expected. He moved to the other side of the rock, almost into the open. The waiting Stefan didn't give him a second chance.

Crouched low, legs apart like some western gunslinger in a Hollywood cowboy movie, the heavy automatic pressed against his right hip to steady it, he squeezed the trigger, taking first pressure. Harry spotted him there. His hands went up to his face, as if he were trying to ward off the bullet with his bare hands. 'No!' he screamed. 'Oh, please, no!' His plea ended with a wild scream of unbearable pain as the bullet tore off his fingers, slammed into his face, shattering it into a bloody gore through which broken bones gleamed like polished ivory. Harry lay there against the rock, gasping his last breaths, choking and drowning in his own blood.

Up ahead, desperately carrying on, knowing that he'd find a hiding place in the end if he kept moving, Chiefie heard that terrible cry and guessed immediately it had come from the poor toothless deserter. 'Bastards!' he gasped, face contorted with hate and bitterness. 'I'll get you . . . By God, I'll make you pay . . .' He staggered on.

Bull was next. The marine deserter had misjudged the distance when he had jumped from the stranded barge. Instead of hitting the shallows, which would have broken his fall, he struck the gravel. It slid beneath his boots. Next instant there was a sharp click, followed by an even sharper red-hot pain which shot through his left leg like electricity. For a minute he was overcome by nausea, and thought he was going to be sick as he crouched there retching. But his crewmate's death cry had made him aware of the danger of his position. He had to go on, broken ankle or not. Desperately he cast around for something to support his weight. He found it in a small plank that had been washed ashore by the raging surf. Slowly and painfully he hobbled away into the darkness, praying that he could find some hiding place before the other killer caught up with him. But his luck was out. Now he had only minutes to live.

Chiefie had cleared the top of the beach. Before him stretched a fertile plain. He had been here before to unload contraband and other illicit cargo. As he remembered the place there was a coastal road that followed the coastline leading towards Palermo a dozen or so kilometres to the north. He knew the two yellow-haired killers had been briefed by Gino, or 'Joe Victory' as he was now beginning to call himself. 'I'm an American, I don't want no wop name!' They knew that their destination was Palermo. Would they assume that he'd attempt to escape in that direction?

For a moment he paused, hands on his knees, his breath coming in sharp hectic gasps, trying to make the right decision. If they did take the coastal road to the Sicilian capital and he did, too, they'd soon catch up with him. They were both younger and a lot fitter than an aged petty officer, whose main diet these last twenty years had mainly consisted of 'the three Ws' – wallop, woods* and women. So the obvious thing to do was to go in the opposite direction. 'And then what?' a hard little voice at the back of his brain asked. 'What yer going to do then, matey, an old crock of a matelot on the beach with a bunch of worthless lire in his duds?'

It was what happened next that would finally decide it for the little deserter, as he started to trot and shamble in the opposition direction to Palermo. Even though the wind continued to howl and the waves crashed and slithered on the beach below, he could hear Bull's voice quite distinctly. Like all marines, Bull was the owner of a very loud voice. Now he was saying menacingly, 'Keep away from me, you wop git . . . or I'll fucking well bash yer brains in with this here stick. Got it?'

His threat received no reply – at first.

Forgetting his own danger for a moment, Chiefie paused and tried to visualize the scene. Perhaps Bull was holding off the gunman with a stick, full of piss and vinegar as most marines were, believing that one marine was as good as half a dozen ordinary English squaddies, and better than a dozen assorted wops, wogs and sundry other foreigners. For a moment Chiefie admired the stupid bastard, facing an armed man with only a stick to defend himself. But his admiration turned to despair the very next moment, as a solitary shot rang out and Bull, his voice angry but full of pain, cried, 'You rotten bastard, you've gorn and shot me in the frigging leg . . .' The cry broke off and there was the sound of someone falling to the ground.

Again Bull spoke, but this time the bravado had vanished from his voice, to be replaced by a weak plea, 'Please don't shoot me like this . . . Please, I don't want—'

A second shot rang out and Bull was silent. One of the yellow-haired killers shouted something in that strange

*Woodbine cigarettes.

113

language they used when together. There was the sound of heavy boots running across the shingle. The chase was on again. Chiefie hesitated no longer. He started to run like he had not run for many a long year, despite the long-term effect of 'the three Ws'. For now he was running for his very life . . .

Six

'Just look at that, Codman!' Patton cried, sweeping the battered horizon with his swagger stick as the guns roared, belching smoke and fire, and the tanks rattled forward, throwing up huge wakes of mud and pebbles. 'Could anything be more magnificent?'

At any other time Colonel Codman would have found his boss's enthusiasm for battle amusing, but not now. Things were far too dangerous up here just behind the fighting front on the Italian mainland.

Their jeep rolled by a grove of skeletal trees, long since swept clean of foliage by constant bombardment, just as a concealed battery of 155mm cannon slammed into action with an ear-shattering salvo. Codman jumped. Patton didn't even show a flicker of fear or surprise. Indeed, the great roar seemed to further increase his excitement at being near the fighting once more. He cupped his hands to his mouth and yelled above the thunder. 'Compared to war, all other forms of human endeavour shrink to insignificance.' His voice shook with emotion. 'God how I love it!'

Codman nodded his understanding, but was not convinced. Indeed it now dawned on him that it had been very dangerous to allow the general to indulge in this pre-Christmas 'treat'. Back in Palermo, Patton had somehow convinced the authorities that he should be sent to Clark's Fifth US Army front on the mainland for a forty-eight hour period. It would give him the opportunity to confer with

Clark, a general who Patton disliked intensely. As he had moaned to Codman more than once, 'Wayne,' he meant Clark, 'tries to be nice to me, but it makes my flesh creep, Codman, to be with him. That jerk Wayne Clark is more preoccupied with bettering his own position than winning the war.' In fact this visit to Clark, who really didn't want to see him, was merely an opportunity for Patton to go to the front once more, after an absence from the fighting zone since the summer. 'Codman,' he had snapped, as they had flown across the Straits of Messina to Naples the day before, 'those bastards in Washington will probably kick me out of the US Army before the year's out. So before I'm put out to pasture, I'd like to see the war for one last time.' And Codman could have sworn that at that moment Patton's hard bitter eyes had suddenly flooded with tears. He had looked away hurriedly, as if embarrassed.

Now, Codman realized, the general was as happy as a sandboy, here at the front once more. Indeed Codman suspected that if Patton had been struck by an enemy shell or bullet at that very moment, he would have died a happy man. He sighed and the jeep rolled on across that bitter wartorn landscape, heading for the forward evacuation where Patton was expected to comfort the wounded, hand out a few medals and, as Eisenhower in London, who had approved Patton's visit, had signalled urgently, '*not cause any more casualties, please.*'

That had made even Patton laugh in a bitter, cynical sort of a way. 'Hell, Codman,' he had exclaimed. 'What does Ike think I do – go around slapping US soldiers all the time!' Then he had let his shoulders slump as if in mock resignation. 'Ike need not worry – Georgie will be a good boy!'

Georgie Patton was. After an exchange of salutes with the medical colonel in charge of the tented hospital, he was told that the tents contained forty wounded who had not yet received their Purple Heart medals and would he, Patton, be kind enough to distribute the medals to the wounded GIs? Patton said he would.

Patton played his new role as if he had rehearsed it for days, Codman thought to himself. It was the same old routine, but Patton seemed to make each little presentation ceremony something special, individual. He'd stop by a bed and ask the wounded soldier: 'Where did you get hit, boy?' The GI would say it was in the chest, leg, arm, and so on. It wasn't important, Patton wouldn't want to see the wound; he didn't like the sight of blood. The question was only to allow him his set address which was, 'Well, it may interest you, son, to know that the last Kraut I saw had no chest (or leg, arm, etc) – and no head either. Get well quick – you want to be in the final kill.'

A beaming Codman told himself that the boss had them all – soldiers, nurses, doctors, usually a hard-boiled bunch – almost weeping, especially when Patton gave the Purple Heart to the last GI to be honoured.

He was unconscious, attached to an oxygen mask, and the attending doctor whispered gravely to Patton, 'We don't think he'll live, sir.'

Patton, like a skilled actor, switched immediately from his warlike stance to that of a concerned, sensitive individual. He took off his helmet, knelt down, pinned the medal to the dying man's pillow, whispered something in his ear and then stood stiffly to attention in salute. The nurses loved it. As they left in the jeep, Patton chuckled and said, 'I guess, Codman, I earned my pay this day and Ike can rest easy, I didn't cause any more *American* casualties.'

An hour later they arrived at Clark's huge headquarters at Caserta to be received by a military band and a guard of honour, which Patton inspected rigorously, his narrow features set in what he called his 'war face number one', the hard military pose that he practised in front of his bedroom mirror virtually every night. But as he returned the commander of the guards' salute with an immaculate one of his own, Codman could see from his flushed cheeks that Patton was very angry. Out of earshot of the honour guard he hissed, 'Where's that son of a bitch, Wayne Clark? He should show enough military courtesy to be here to welcome me, the bastard. This is a calculated, deliberate insult. The big bastard is jealous. He knows I can out-fight him any frigging time. Now that I'm in disgrace and out in the cold, he's trying to rub my nose in the crap—'

'General, General,' Codman interrupted him urgently. '*Please*. Someone might hear you.'

'I don't frigging care if they do . . . Doesn't that bastard want to show some respect for my past and my white hair?' He slapped his swagger cane hard against the side of his highly polished riding boot, as if in his mind he was giving the hated Clark a great whack across the behind.

It was about then that an aide approached, a fat colonel with jowls, who had the knowing face of a small-town fixer, a provincial petty crook of the kind that the Bostonian Codman had known and disliked all his pre-war working life. Now he was decked out in a custom-tailored uniform, probably made in London, complete with expensive leather paratrooper boots, which he was not entitled to wear, and a leather swagger cane of the type carried by General Patton himself. Codman took an unreasonable and instant dislike to him.

The colonel tucked his cane beneath his right arm in the British fashion and swung Patton a tremendous salute, as if he were straight out of West Point, barking in a whisky-soaked, gravelly voice, 'General Clark presents his compliments and apologizes for the delay. He wonders, sir, if you would like to partake of a little liquid refreshment in the meantime, sir?'

Patton looked down disdainfully at the fat, sweating

colonel in his Bond Street uniform and Codman knew what was coming. He tensed. 'Of course I'd like a *fucking* drink, Colonel – a very big *fucking* drink!'

The colonel looked startled. Obviously he wasn't accustomed to being addressed in this fashion even from three-star generals. He stuttered, 'Would the general be kind enough to follow me, sir. I shall attend to it immediately.' He set off, his fat behind wobbling in the too-tight light brown pants, while behind him Patton winked at Codman and said, so that the fat colonel couldn't help but overhear, 'These guys of the Fifth Army live high on the hog, Codman. I think Wayne ought to be advised to make 'em shape up. A week or two in the line on C rations and no fattening booze should do the trick.'

Codman did not answer. He was too busy praying that his boss wouldn't put his foot in it with Clark and his HQ staff. The old man had enough strikes against him already. If Ike were ever again to employ him in an active command in Europe, Patton had better keep his nose clean. Somehow, however, he thought his boss wouldn't. He was right.

'My American Eagle', Churchill had called Wayne Clark when he and Ike had first been sent to take over in London back in '42. Indeed he did have the facial features of an eagle – long face, great beak of a nose and dangerous-looking eyes. When Patton had heard of Churchill's remark he had quipped, 'More like a goddam American vulture in my opinion.' His bitterness was understandable, Codman thought now, for although Clark was ten years younger than Patton and had spent exactly an hour in the front line in the 'Old War', wounded as he was going into the trenches for the first time, the former was obviously on the way up while he, Patton, seemed to be on his way out.

Watching the top generals now, as they sat down for dinner in the great echoing dining room, balancing themselves on the silk upholstered chairs designed for small Italians and not six foot tall, heavy US top brass, Codman could see his boss was already regarded by Clark's staff as virtually a has-been. The days were gone when a mere glance from Patton, a gesture, the lifting of a glass or cigar would have had them hurrying to offer him food, more wine, a light. When Patton now attempted to tell one of his celebrated and profane tales, known and liked throughout the US Regular Army, they didn't listen. Instead, their attention was fixed slavishly on General Clark and his senior generals.

For a while Codman felt for his boss. He was trying to be on his best behaviour, almost as if he had been humbled by the events of recent weeks, trying to curry favour, however much it went against the grain. Yet his attempts to do so were doomed. General Ole Blood an' Guts Patton was seemingly of no future importance to these Johnny-come-latelys of Clark's Fifth Army. So he would be sent back to the States under a shadow. He'd retire, destined to become a footnote in the history of World War Two.

Patton, half way through the dinner, was talking excitedly about his summer campaign in Sicily, making the point that it hadn't been Monty and his famous Eighth Army that had won the day, but his own Seventh which had fought the decisive battles. 'By God,' he exclaimed, his thin face flushed with too much wine. 'Don't the folks back home realize that we took on Hitler's elite troops, the Hermann Goering Division, and beat the shit outa them, while the British fought only wops!'

The fat colonel with the jowls who had received them an hour or so before said, 'With all due respect, General, we don't call our new Italian allies – er – wops at this HQ.' He looked at General Clark as if seeking his approval.

Clark nodded and said, 'Yeah, Georgie, you'll have to get with the programme, you know. We're going to need the new Italian army up there in the mountains if we're gonna win. We'd better stop calling 'em names, eh Georgie.'

Patton flushed an even deeper red. Codman tensed. Was his boss going to blow up, cause a scene as he'd done so often in the old days, when he had commanded an army? But Patton was learning. Slowly he rose from the table, crumpled his napkin and dropped it. He pushed back his chair quietly, gave a kind of bow in the direction of Clark and his top brass. If he expected a reaction from Clark, he was disappointed. For the Fifth Army commander merely said, 'Want to make an early night of it, Georgie? I expect it's been a tiring day for you – at your age.'

Codman tensed again. It was a calculated insult. Was the boss going to explode now? But again Patton kept his temper. 'Yes, Wayne, I expect you're right,' he answered softly. He nodded to Codman, who rose immediately. 'Good night, gentlemen,' he called as he reached the great door of the eighteenth-century dining room.

No one responded, but the fat colonel with the jowls gave a little laugh. To Codman it sounded like one of triumph. But in his emotional state at that moment, he told himself, he might well have been mistaken.

Next morning they were back at Naples field. This time there was no guard of honour or band to bid the ex-Seventh Army commander farewell, just a couple of sleepy MPs, the local Army Air Corps base commander, and the fat colonel with the jowls, whom Codman had grown to hate, though he didn't even know the man's name.

Hands were shaken, salutes exchanged, 'Happy Christmas' uttered. Then they were seated in the freezing C-47, its engines roaring so that conversation was virtually impossible. The general's face was stoney. He didn't look down at the pathetic little crowd standing there waiting impatiently for the plane to take off so that they could get back to the warmth of their billets. If Patton *had* looked, he might have noted the broken-down Italian with the wooden leg standing at the perimeter watching the C-47 begin to roll for take-off with much more interest than any of the American spectators. But Patton continued to stare straight ahead while Codman, sitting next to him, felt for his boss. At that moment he looked like an enfeebled old man. Indeed as the plane commenced its take-off with a great roar of engines he shouted to Codman, all pride and hope vanished now, 'Christ, Charley, why didn't those assassins shoot me that day!'

It was a statement that almost broke Codman's heart.

SECTION THREE
Vile Murder

One

'Well, sir,' the young American naval lieutenant said, nursing his wounded arm which was now in a sling, 'our mission was to stop this illegal smuggling between the mainland and Sicily. But we didn't expect this kind of deal.' He pointed to the rusty keel of the landing craft being washed by the tide. 'The bastards got the skipper and two of the crew.' He shrugged, then winced at the sudden pain in his arm and wished he hadn't. 'As for the boat, I think the Navy will have to scrap her.'

Mackenzie nodded his understanding as Campbell walked thoughtfully to where the body of the Royal Marine had been found and picked up two empty cartridge cases to stare at them in silence. 'Where did you get your intelligence about these smugglers?' Mackenzie asked.

'Just by chance, sir,' the young lieutenant answered. 'We kept hearing of this limey – er,' he flushed red, 'British landing craft running back and forth across the Straits of Messina, but we couldn't identify the outfit to which it belonged.'

'I see. Well, what do you think this mysterious limey – ' he allowed himself a mild grin and the lieutenant blushed even more – 'barge carried as cargo?'

'Our naval intelligence guys thought it might just be black market stuff stolen from our supply depots on the mainland. There's a lot of that kind of thing. You know the wops have long fingers. But there's something else too.' He fumbled inside his sling and brought out a small package with his good hand. 'I was told to give you this, sir.'

'What is it?' Mackenzie asked, taking the package.

'Intelligence says it's cocaine, sir.'

'Cocaine! You mean *drug smuggling*?'

'Yessir. And that worries our people a lot. The intelligence guys say if drug smuggling is the name of the game, then the Mafia are involved.'

Mackenzie considered for a moment before saying slowly, 'But I thought your naval intelligence wallahs had the Mafia under control? It was naval intelligence that brought the Mafia back to Italy in the first place.'

The young American officer was embarrassed again. 'I don't know anything about that, sir. All I know is that I hope you'll catch the bastards who killed the skipper and the other guys.'

'Of course we will,' Mackenzie said, though he didn't know how exactly this new Mafia business was any concern of his or how it affected their mission to protect Patton before he was sent to London. He raised his voice and said confidently, as if he had everything under control, which he definitely didn't, 'Now you get back to the warmth of the peep*, while we have a further look around here. Then we'll take you back to Palermo. You've been a great help. Off you go.'

'Thank you, sir.' The American shuffled awkwardly to attention in the wet sand and gravel and then went back to the waiting vehicle on the tight coastal road above the beach.

'I'm puzzled,' Mackenzie said. 'I really must confess . . . I'm up the proverbial creek without a paddle. If this is a Mafia thing, it might have something to do with our problem. And again, if it's a Mafia thing, how come

*A covered jeep.

126

American naval intelligence have lost control over their nasty little protégés, eh?'

'Because the second thug on the picture you – er – *found*,' Campbell said discreetly, 'this Joe Victory, has disappeared, sir. And he was US naval intelligence's main contact with the Mafia.'

'You mean this business with the barge had something to do with Joe Victory and he's decided to lie low for a while till the heat's off, Campbell?'

'That's my guess, sir, especially now that the Yanks have found out about this cocaine. US naval intelligence men might be pragmatists, but they won't want to get involved with drugs.' He chuckled. 'Perhaps they've got rid of Joe Victory themselves. So far the Yanks haven't been scared of getting their fingers dirty. Now with the drug business, who knows . . . Dead men don't tell tales.'

Mackenzie stared at the winter seascape, bleak and bare, feeling just as bleak himself. 'You know, Campbell, there are so many leads in this case, yet none of them seem to lead to a satisfactory conclusion. Now we've got drug smuggling, two dead British sailors, or a marine and a sailor, both deserters . . .'

'And one, we suspect, still alive plus two others, who we might classify as unknowns . . . well, almost unknown.'

For a moment Mackenzie was too concerned with the new mystery to note Campbell's qualifying statement. 'Yes,' he agreed. 'Three sets of footprints higher on the beach where the tide couldn't get at them. So that means that there were five men aboard that barge when she came in. Two down, as it were, and three to go.' Breaking off his train of thought abruptly, he snapped, 'What did you mean when you said *almost unknown*, Campbell?'

By way of an answer, Campbell opened his gloved hand to reveal the cartridge cases he had picked up a few yards away from the beached barge. 'These, sir.'

'So?'

'Well, firstly they're nine millimetre bullets.'

'I can see that. So?'

'Well, neither the British Army nor the Yanks use weapons which fire nine millimetre bullets.'

'Go on.'

'Take a look at the base of this one, sir. You can see the writing quite clearly.' Campbell held up the slug for Mackenzie's inspection and, squinting against the wind coming off the sea, the latter read, *'Fabrik Nummer 122.'* He whistled softly as he said the German number of the ammunition batch aloud. 'Hun, eh?'

'Exactly, sir,' Campbell said, amused at Mackenzie's use of the word 'Hun'. 'So why and how were the men who killed the marine and the other poor old sod armed with weapons that used German ammunition? Where would the Mafia – if that's who the killers were, and I think they were – get German weapons?'

For a while Mackenzie didn't have an answer to that question. Like everything connected with the Patton business, just when it seemed they had a solution, a fresh mystery or problem arose. So the two of them plodded back to the waiting peep in a heavy silence broken only by the howl of the wind and the subdued sound of the sea.

Just before they reached the waiting vehicle, the driver already gunning his engine as if he couldn't get away from this remote place quickly enough, Mackenzie stopped and grabbed Campbell's arm urgently. 'Let us assume, Campbell, that these Mafia types are working for both sides, the Americans *and* the Germans. That might make some sense perhaps?'

'Not altogether, sir, to be honest with you,' Campbell answered. 'But sir, let's not go into that for a moment. As I see it, we're still punching in the dark, as it were. Giggles, we know, is dead. Joe Victory has slung his hook, vanished for the time being. Two of the men who did the killing with those German bullets have vanished. If they have Mafia connections they'll have well and truly gone to ground. We'll never find 'em in those Sicilian mountain villages where the Mafia usually hides out. None of the villagers up there would dare to give them away, and the Eyetie civvie police are scared shitless of tackling the mountain villages. *If* that's where our two killers are.'

'Agreed, Sergeant. Go on – tell me how to do my business,' Mackenzie added without rancour, for he was full of admiration for his new German-Jewish colleague. Campbell had the gift of the gab. His statements were extremely logical and he possessed an expert power of reasoning.

'Sorry, sir,' Campbell apologized hastily. 'I didn't mean to be pushy or talk out of turn. But I feel the only person we've got at the moment – or to put it better, haven't got yet but should find as soon as possible – is that third unknown, the one that the two killers failed to get rid of. He ought to talk. After all, the Mafia types with the German weapons killed his two pals in cold blood. He's got a grudge . . . I hope.'

Mackenzie stroked his chin thoughtfully. 'You're right. He's our best bet at this moment – and remember if these chaps, whoever they are, are going to try and bump off our Yank general, they're going to do it at that Christmas party with the palazzo wide open.' The sudden eager look in Mackenzie's hard eyes died as abruptly as it had appeared. 'But where are we going to find this unknown, eh?'

Campbell 175 grinned. 'If I may say so, where do you expect a sailor to go at a time like this?'

Mackenzie shared his grin. 'I know . . . I know!' he chortled, suddenly feeling they were getting somewhere at last. 'Heaven help a sailor on a night like this, what? *The knocking shops*!'

'Natch, sir! What better place to take a dive with no questions asked except how much money you've got, sailor, and is that a revolver you've got in yer pocket, or do you love me, sailor!'

Laughing uproariously the two young men ran back the remaining few yards to the waiting peep, while the American driver and the wounded young naval officer watched them, thinking they had suddenly gone crazy while the officer told himself everybody knew the limeys were all loco. It was something to do with all that tea they drank . . .

Two

C hiefie was drunk, or at least he appeared to be drunk. Staggering through the door, down the darkened steps, pushing the little Italian bouncer to one side with an imperious, 'Make way there for a naval officer!' he came to stop in the middle of the bar room and cried, for no particular reason: 'Crap, said the Lord and a thousand arseholes bent and took the strain. For in them days the word of the Lord—' The rest of his words were drowned by the laughter of the painted whores and a flourish on the drums by the drummer in the corner, followed by a long chord from the accordionist.

'*Ciao . . . buona sera . . . quanto*?' Chiefie rattled off the three phrases double quick and, as if to make his intentions quite clear, he pulled a handful of dollar bills from his pocket and threw them into the air, which occasioned an unladylike scramble from the whores, for the illegal dollar was worth a fortune in lire.

The little naval deserter swayed alarmingly and then gave his silly gap-toothed grin. By gum, look at the flanks on that tart – bigger than a Clydesdale mare – and them tits on that one. Blimey, you could get yer head trapped in between them and a bloke couldn't hear a thing for a fortnight. He laughed uproariously and swayed dangerously again as the Madame pushed her way through the whores who were on their knees, fighting and giggling in their attempts to get their red-tipped fingers on the precious dollars. She carried her enormous breasts before her, as if on a silver tray to be offered to the highest bidder.

She gave the drunken sailor her professional fake smile. 'You like nice girl, Tommy?' she asked.

He swayed again and said, 'No, *bad* girl . . . and not just one but two.' He held up his fingers to make it quite clear. '*Duo . . . Claro*?'

'*Two*?'

He grabbed the front of his dirty overalls and said roguishly. 'Bin at sea a long time, missus. Got a lotta heavy water to get off my manly chest. *Two*!' He slapped the huge bottom of the whore he'd compared to a Clydesdale mare and chortled, 'I'll have her for starters. Good solid tart – she ought to be able to stand a lot . . .' He grinned inanely at the Madame. 'Drunk as a skunk I am, but I'm generous, Florrie. I can pay for everything.' He opened his breast pocket to reveal the thick wad of dollars resting there. 'Play yer cards right, Florrie, and I might even slip you a link.' He pressed her right nipple which was protruding through the tight black silk of her blouse. 'By hellus, you've got a right pair o' tits there, Florrie.'

The Madame took it all in her stride. She had been thirty years in the business. She knew sailors and their habits. As long as they paid up in advance and didn't wreck the furniture, her establishment was 'liberty hall', as the English called it. '*Prego*,' she said. 'You want two o' my ladies. You pay fifteen dollars for each one time . . . or forty for both all night. *Claro*?'

'*Claro*.' With apparent carelessness, Chiefie peeled off two twenty dollar bills and handed them to the Madame with a drunken flourish. 'Stuff that up yer stocking, Florrie. Perhaps I can get me pinkies up there later and all – *for free*.'

'Florrie' smiled but made no comment. Under his breath, Chiefie muttered, 'Wouldn't give yer the muck from under

132

her nails, that old bag wouldn't.' Aloud he said happily, 'Come on then, girlies. Come to old Chiefie and let the dog see the frigging cat. Ha. ha!'

He put his arms around the two giggling whores and winked. 'I shall now retire with my darlings. Don't wake me till dawn tomorrow.' The whores had absolutely no idea what the wrinkled old sailor was talking about. It didn't matter. They admired his spirit and vigour and, in particular, the Yankee dollars he was throwing about so generously. They clapped.

Chiefie gave a little bow and then, supported – or so it seemed – by the two ladies of the night, he started to clamber up the rickety wooden stairs to the bedrooms, singing wildly:

'Drunk last night . . .
Drunk the night before . . .
Gonna get drunk tonight like I've never bin drunk
    before . . .
We're all good pals and jolly good company . . .'

But once out of sight, as the whores opened the door of the sordid little bedroom, he stopped singing, his act over. He'd done it. He'd got a place for the night, he'd taken a dive. He gave a sigh of relief. For the time being he was safe from the Mafia killers, or whoever those blond bastards were.

On the bed, the skinny whore was pulling off her knickers, ready to release the 'Clydesdale mare' from her corset. He whistled softly through the gap in his front teeth and cried, 'Luvverly grub! . . . Now come on, darlings. Don't waste no more time. Old lover boy here has got a lot of time to make up for.'

Five minutes later, his worries forgotten for a while, he was busily engaged beneath the grubby sheets, working out the complicated procedures of making love to two women at the same time and enjoying every minute of it . . .

The Palermo dockfront was almost silent now. The cranes, derricks and other machinery had long ceased working. The curfew was now fully in force, which meant that both civilians and military had to be off the streets. Occasionally a lone jeep cruised by, filled with 'white mice', as the Italians called the white-helmeted American military police. Outside the harbour, in the Straits, there came the occasional mournful howl of a ship's siren as the fog crept in once more. Otherwise everything was muted, damp, somehow sad, as if the wet mist had cast a cloak of gloom over the Sicilian capital city.

Still, the fog and the curfew suited Mackenzie. He knew that anyone still on the street was potentially suspect and could be arrested on sight. He knew, too, that behind those tightly shuttered Sicilian waterfront dives, there was a life of sorts – sordid, vicious, nasty, fuelled by lust and avarice. For here in Palermo in this wartime Christmas week of 1943, you could buy everything and anybody for money. He told himself that it made a mockery of what they were supposed to be fighting for – a better world. In the end the old vices and the old greeds would triumph, as they always did. It was the nature of the beast.

Quietly, their engines now switched off, the little convoy of jeeps rolled to a stop on the dripping, blacked-out quay. On the opposite side of the cobbled road lay the illegal drinking dens and knocking shops. Here and there Mackenzie caught a glimpse of a chink of light, which was forbidden. The blackout was still strictly enforced in Palermo, despite the fact that the war on the mainland had moved much further north. Now the rumble of permanent barrage could no longer be heard over the Straits of Messina. Palermo had returned to peace.

He gave a soft signal. The MPs and the Italian police got out of their jeeps. Campbell whispered quiet instructions in his fluent Italian. They began to spread out. As they crossed towards the sordid brothels and bars, Mackenzie could hear the faint sound of muted dance music. It indicated that they were still inside there – people who must not be disturbed in advance in case they raised the alarm. Then all hell would break loose and the men who had a price on their heads – the mafiosi, Allied deserters, perhaps even drug dealers – would be running in ten different directions and they'd lose the man they really sought.

Next to him, Campbell took out his revolver, released the safety catch and checked the chamber. Automatically Mackenzie did the same. The people inside those shuttered houses were desperate men. There was no telling what they might do, trapped like rats as they were.

They continued their silent advance, the only sound outside the lap-lap of water in the harbour and the drip-drip of wet mist from the cranes and roofs. Now the MPs and the Italian police moved in two groups to the end of the street. On Mackenzie's signal they would close in from left and right and begin searching the houses. If the occupants refused to open up then the police, armed with sledgehammers, would begin breaking down the doors, while the US military policemen would slip round the back and wait for the fugitives to try to escape.

Campbell, close to Mackenzie, whispered, 'It's like a Gestapo *Nacht-und-Nebel* action, sir, isn't it? It happened to me once.'

Mackenzie didn't like the comparison. 'This is none of your secret police night and fog deals, Campbell,' he hissed severely. 'We're doing nothing illegal. It's those crooked bastards inside who are the ones doing something illegal.'

'Sorry, sir,' Campbell whispered, a little crestfallen. He thought the major had been in a good mood for the last forty-eight hours since they had begun to follow the tracks of the unknowns who had escaped from the wrecked barge. He'd been mistaken. Perhaps he was having trouble with the girl, Adriana.

'Forget it,' Mackenzie ordered. 'Let's get on with it.' They moved on again.

At the door of the central house, which Mackenzie knew from the police was a brothel catering mostly for Allied sailors, but which had a reputation for trading drugs – in particular the new penicillin, stolen from the American military hospitals still located on the island – the major checked to left and right. Through the misty gloom he could see that both parties were in position at either end of the street. He nodded his approval. He whispered to Campbell, 'Tell Angelo here to get ready with his axe.' He indicated the burly Italian policeman standing behind him. 'Just in case they've locked the door.'

Campbell translated while Mackenzie, head cocked to one side to hear better, could hear the rusty squeak of bedsprings working overtime, going at it like a fiddler's elbow as they'd quipped when he had first joined the British Army in what now seemed like another world. Campbell finished. Mackenzie wasted no more time. He raised his whistle to his lips and blew three short, sharp blasts.

Suddenly, startlingly, everything was rapid action. Men shouted. Police hammered on doors. Cries of alarm. The sound of heavy boots running. In the jeeps the drivers broke blackout regulations. They focused their spots on the facades of the waterfront dives. Someone tried to slip out of a window.

'Hold it there, buddy!' a harsh American voice commanded. The man tried to keep going. Not for long. A white club descended on the back of his skull. He hit the wet gleaming cobbles without even a moan.

Now doors were being unlocked and unbarred. Angry

startled civilians came into the glaring spotlights, shielding their eyes against the dazzle. Cries of protest. A woman, half-naked, her breasts jutting out in front of her like a ships prow demanded, '*Porco di Madonna* . . . Whata you want, eh?'

Here and there the Italian police started battering on the unopened door with the brass butts of their rifles. Someone sloshed a chamber pot's contents over the policemen's heads. Angry cries of rage and revenge. A shot rang out. And another. The Italians were rattled. Mackenzie shouted at Campbell, waiting to examine the inhabitants' papers as they started to file out under the watchful gaze of the US military policemen swinging their white clubs threateningly as they towered above the smaller Sicilians. 'Tell them to cease firing, Campbell . . . For God's sake!'

Campbell did so. The firing stopped. Now the pimps, the brothel madames, the whores, and all the rest of the port's riff-raff came out into the open, shivering either with fear or the change in temperature. From within the dives came the fetid smell of sweat, sex and sin. Mackenzie wrinkled his nose in disgust. 'The human condition,' he told himself. 'And as usual, completely shitty!' He dismissed the thought and concentrated on watching the MPs and their new Italian allies examine the various documents that were being produced, accompanied by the usual protests, complaints and much waving of hands.

But old hand that he was, Mackenzie knew that in these dives nobody was what he seemed to be; papers could be forged or bought. So he flashed each individual a glance, knowing that he was looking for a northern European, probably another Englishman like the two who had been murdered on the beach two days before. And Englishmen, he told himself, were hard to disguise, even if they did wear foreign clothes and speak the local language.

But this particular Englishman seemed to be absent from

the dives this morning. Perhaps they were all back at sea, supporting the new coastal landing at Anzio; he had heard that things were going badly for the Anglo-American task force which had assaulted the beaches there. Indeed only one client of the first brothel they tackled admitted to being English. He was a great black stoker from the Merchant Navy, drunk as a lord and wearing a battered bowler, though the rest of his gigantic frame was half-clothed. He cried when he saw the British uniform, 'Hey, you English? Them Yanks can never beat us English.' He flashed a startled Mackenzie a brilliant-white drunken smile in the same instant one of the American MPs gave him a great whack across the back of his shaven skull with the command, 'Shut your black trash mushmouth, nigger!'

Just as Mackenzie was beginning to think the raid had been a failure, at least for him – the truck they had brought for other types of wanted persons was already full of glum, drunk or protesting petty criminals – the trouble commenced. They had about worked their way to the end of the row of dives, silhouetted in the harsh white glare of the spotlights, when a surprised cry went up from a group of American MPs. 'There's a guy on the roof! Hey! There's a guy up there to the right. D'ya see him?'

Mackenzie and Campbell shot a glance upwards as one of the spots illuminated a man crouched near the crown of the roof, pinned down by the harsh light like a dead insect on some collector's card. Instinctively they knew they had a suspect, for both caught a glimpse of the man's yellow hair, which indicated he was no *Siciliano*.

'Don't let him get away, you jerks!' the big lieutenant in charge of the MPs yelled. 'Can't you see that he's—'

'*Stop!*' Mackenzie cried frantically.

Too late. On one of the jeeps the vehicle's half-inch burst into angry life. White tracer zipped upwards in a lethal Morse code. In a graceful curve, gathering speed by the instant, it descended upon the roof. Slates shattered, glass tinkled and broke. The yellow-haired man screamed – a long, high, hysterical scream that seemed to go on for ever. Next moment the man plunged over the edge of the roof in a spectacular dive to hit the cobbles below with a nauseating crunch. There he lay still in the sudden silence, in a circle of hard white light, while the echo of that burst of deadly fire died away into the distance of the night.

Three

'Old shipmate,' Chiefie whispered to himself – like all lonely men, he tended to talk to himself – 'if you don't watch out, they're gonna get yer by the short and curlies.' He was perched on the top of the crane overlooking the tense little scene on the quay below.

The American MPs had taken their prisoners away, leaving a handful of them grouped around the dead body sprawled in a star of blood on the cobbles, the lights of their jeeps directed at the two men in British battledress bending over the corpse.

Quick-witted as all cockneys are, the deserter sized up the scene immediately. The Yanks and the two fellows in British uniforms had been looking for those who had survived the shooting on the beach. 'And that includes yours truly,' he said to himself as the wind howled high up on the top of the crane. The rozzers hadn't found him – yet. But they had found the yellow-haired bugger who had shot his crew. He was dead, fortunately, so he couldn't blab. But there was another of them out there somewhere and that spelled trouble for Chiefie.

He shivered as he clung to the slightly swaying girder. Not because he felt any sense of vertigo – as a boy sailor at King Alfred's he'd climbed higher masts than this in his bare feet – but because he was cold. He had just had time to slip on his shoes and dungarees when the rozzers had started to beat down the door of the knocking shop. Underneath the overalls he was naked, and the wind was bleeding perishing, as he said to himself.

Below, the English soldier with the white-painted sergeant's stripes on the arm of his battledress blouse was examining the corpse more closely and, for a moment, Chiefie wished he could be closer to the scene; he'd dearly love to know what the two English investigators would find out, if anything. For Chiefie realized that his own fate might well be decided by what they discovered about the yellow-haired killer. Who *was* the bastard? He wasn't Italian, that was for sure. He had worked for that wop Joe Victory, or whatever his moniker was. But did that mean he belonged to the Mafia? Somehow Chiefie didn't think he did. The Mafia thugs didn't usually engage in fire with a US patrol boat. So who was the dead man, really?

Chiefie wiped a dewdrop off the end of his pinched red nose and slung it into the darkness. 'A lot of ruddy questions,' he whispered to himself, 'but ruddy few bleeding answers.'

Sixty feet below on the wet quay, surrounded by the silent, gum-chewing Yank MPs, Mackenzie felt the same. As Campbell gingerly started to examine the body more closely, he was sure that the dead man was one of those who had escaped from the beached landing craft. He must have been one of the two who had fired the shots which killed the two British deserters. But the man didn't look at all like Mackenzie expected a Mafia killer to look. He was far too tall and blond for an Italian, even for one from the north of the country. But if the dead man wasn't a mafioso, who was he? Why was he hiding out in a brothel? And where was the other yellow-haired killer? But above all, a frustrated impatient Mackenzie asked himself, had he any connection with the plot to kill old Patton?

It was about then, when Mackenzie was just about to voice his questions to Sergeant Campbell, that the latter looked up and said urgently, 'Sir, would you like to come and have a look at this?'

The note of urgency in the young NCO's voice stopped Mackenzie from asking for an explanation there and then. Instead he did as requested. He stepped a few paces forward and bent to see what his sergeant had discovered.

Campbell had rolled the dead man's sleeve up for some reason to reveal a brawny, muscular left arm. Now he turned the arm slightly outwards so that Mackenzie could see the inner flesh. 'Look a bit closer, sir, if you would,' Campbell urged as the man controlling the spotlight in the nearest jeep called, 'Get outa the way, guys. Let the dog see the cat, willya!'

Obediently the silent, gum-chewing military policemen did so, while the Italian police, like all Italians afraid of the dead in case their spirits came back to haunt them, hurriedly did the same. Now the light was focused directly on the corpse's upper body and its bare arm. Gingerly Campbell raised it so that now Mackenzie could see the marks tattooed on the paler flesh of the inner part. For a moment he was puzzled till Campbell enlightened him. 'SS, sir,' he announced solemnly. 'Saw this a lot, sir, when I was with field intelligence back with the old Kiwis and—'

'*SS?*' Mackenzie interrupted him sharply. 'How do you know, Campbell?'

'A, that's the dead chap's blood group, sir. Only the SS have their blood group marked on their arm like that. The *Wehrmacht* doesn't. Nor the *Kriegsmarine*.' He meant the German Navy.

Mackenzie whistled softly. 'And that other mark. The one that looks like a W in that pseudo-Runic script the Nazis use?'

Campbell allowed himself a slight smile despite the circumstances on this cold, pre-dawn December day. 'Very interesting, sir. The letter marks the fact that the stiff once belonged to Germany's most elite *Waffen* SS regiment – SS *Wotan*.'

'And what is this *"Wotan"* when it's at home?' Mackenzie demanded. He had mysteries enough on his hands – there had been nothing *but* bloody mysteries, ever since they had been sent by Monty to Sicily. He didn't want any more.

'*Reichsführer* SS's toughest and, I have to say, bravest regimental formation. They call themselves the "Führer's fire brigade" because whenever there's a serious problem at the front, a breakthrough, a forced German retreat and the like, they're rushed off to deal with it, to put out the fire. Just when I was ordered to report to you at Eighth Army HQ, the Kiwis – you know, the New Zealand Division – were having one hell of job trying to break through *Wotan*'s front . . .'

Mackenzie wasn't listening any more. His mind was already fully engaged trying to digest and assess this new piece of information, and it was proving damnably difficult for him to do so. Again it seemed that every new lead took them up a blind alley.

After a moment he gave up and asked hopefully, 'Have you found anything else, Campbell, that might help us with, well you know what?' He didn't want to reveal anything about the Patton business to the Yank MPs, and especially not to the Eyetie cops. Policemen, in his experience, were great gossips when they felt they were safe among their own kind.

'Well, we've got his pistol, sir. I'm sure it'll match the bullet cases I found on the beach.'

'That's something,' Mackenzie said slowly. 'So we've got one killer still on the loose and one Briton – and I presume the missing sailor is British – still on the run.' He pursed his lips. He had made up his mind. 'Right, we continue our search for the two missing blokes. In the meantime, let's seal this place off and then get back to the hotel. I need a hot drink, preferably one well laced with rum, even if it's that rotgut Eyetie stuff.'

'Couldn't agree with you more, sir,' Campbell said heartily. He'd had enough of the cold quayside himself. He took one last look at the mysterious dead SS man. Then he kicked him savagely in the ribs and muttered something in German. Mackenzie shook his head, but said nothing. He understood Campbell's motives. Besides, they were living in a crazy world where casual brutality was a everyday occurrence . . .

Up in his hiding place on the girder Chiefie relaxed at last. The jeeps had vanished. Now the corpse lay there in its red star of blood, abandoned, save for the frightened Italian policeman who kept his distance, as if he didn't trust the dead man. Again he spat into the night; he didn't know why. Perhaps it was nerves; perhaps he just felt the desire to spit. His brain was racing. The heat was off. But it would be on again soon enough, he knew that. It was important then that he made his decision *now* about what he was going to do next. Tomorrow would be too late.

He longed for a fag, but that was impossible. The little frightened dago cop below might spot him. He had to stick it out in the freezing wind, make a decision, and then do a bunk under the cover of the remaining darkness. For in an hour or so, he knew, it would be the sudden, startling Mediterranean dawn.

He pursed his lips, brow creased as he thought out his options. He could give himself up. That would ensure he'd be safe from the Mafia and the remaining yellow-haired killer. But if he did, he'd be court-martialled for desertion and in the Med the courts were particularly severe; there were too many deserters in Italy, especially now as the winter grew harder and the fighting up in the mountains tougher. 'Don't fancy spending a couple of years in the glasshouse,' he whispered to himself. 'No fags, no booze, all a bloke's got to look forward to is a crafty wank under the blankets after lights out – that's if a bloke's got the strength to bash the bishop in them places.'

He dismissed the idea of surrender. There had to be another way: one that would ensure he'd be safe from the military authorities and the Mafia killers. But what was it?

For a while he just clung there in the wind, trying to sort the puzzle out, already aware that to the east it was growing lighter, heralding the start of a new day. It was about then that he was startled out of his reverie by the sound of a ship's siren out in the Straits. Automatically he swung round. Like all old salts, the sea and its activities always aroused his interest, made him forget other things.

There, perhaps half a mile off land, there was a blaze of lights, moving steadily towards the harbour. For one long moment he couldn't take it in. All those lights in wartime. That skipper deserved to get a tin fish up his arse from the nearest Jerry U-boat! Then he understood. He saw the gleaming white of the ship's side, emblazoned with a great red cross. Of course, it was a hospital ship bringing in the latest wounded and sick from the front on the mainland. The Yanks always brought the more serious casualties to the relative peace of Sicily.

Chiefie's wizened old face suddenly lit up. His new plan came to him there and then, and it was one hundred per cent perfect. Of course, that was his way out of here. He'd seen these hospital ships come in before, back in the old days in Alex when the Eighth Army had been fighting their way up and down the coastline of Egypt, Libya, etc month in, month out.

The hospital ship would dock at first light, when there'd be few prying eyes about to witness the number of sick and wounded men, or spread rumours about the misery

and squalor of the sick. Such things were bad for the
morale of the rest of the troops. Waiting for the ship at
the dock would be scores of stretcher-bearers, medics and
ambulances, motors already running, to whip the wounded
and sick straight off to the hospitals before Alexandria really
woke up.

Everything would be done in a tremendous rush: a quick
glance at the label attached to each man's tunic, a check
on the amount of morphine pencilled in on the man's
forehead, a swift going over with the MO's stethoscope
of any suddenly unconscious man's heart, and then it
would be: '*Move it . . . easy there . . . At the double
now . . . Get yer ruddy finger out, you stretcher-bearers!*'
And the dock would be cleared in double-quick time.
There'd be no time wasted on asking questions or probing
examinations. As long as a bloke seemed to be croaking
there and then and had some sort of wound label on
him or other indication that he was sick, no questions
were asked.

Chiefie made up his mind, as outside the white-painted
hospital ship started to sound its siren urgently. It was the
signal intended to alert the stretcher-bearers, ambulance
drivers, doctors and nurses that she was now coming in
to discharge her cargo of misery and evidence of man's
inhumanity to fellow man. It was time to go.

Like a monkey he began to swing his way down from
the top of crane, dropping expertly from girder to girder
as if he were still that fourteen-year-old barefoot boy who
had climbed up and down the masts on *HMS Drake* when
he had been a patriotic child. A child who had believed in
the King-Emperor, 'all that red on the map', and above all,
in His Majesty's Senior Service.

Lightly he dropped to the quayside, looked to left and
right. All was clear. The lone Italian policeman guarding the
spot where the yellow-haired man had died had not heard

him. Chiefie grinned and told himself they'd have to get up a lot earlier if they wanted to catch Mrs Reynolds' handsome son. He spat again. A moment later he had vanished into the new dawn.

Four

'The boss is feeling very low,' Codman said in a hushed tone, as he indicated to Mackenzie the tall erect figure of Patton standing near the window and staring out into the gardens of his palazzo HQ. 'I can't seem to get anything cheerful out of him.'

Mackenzie nodded, but made no comment. He had come to admire Patton; at least he looked like a stark contrast to most US general officers he had met, who seemed more like overweight businessmen dressed, for some inexplicable reason, in military uniform.

'I'm trying to get him interested in this Christmas party we're putting on for the locals and the kids.' He shrugged. 'No deal. The boss just won't play ball. This inactivity and uncertainty is too much for him.'

For a moment Mackenzie was tempted to tell Codman, who he liked, that in the coming year Patton would be called to the UK to take over an army under the Supreme Commander. But he resisted the temptation. The Yanks, he had discovered, were great gossips. It was better to keep that kind of information to himself. So he asked instead, 'Would you fill me in on the plan for the Christmas celebrations?'

'Sure, come along to my room. I've got it all worked out.'

Together they strode down the broad echoing corridor, both walls hung with eighteen and nineteenth-century portraits of Italian worthies who looked down their noses, as

148

though in disdain at these Anglo-Saxon upstarts who were now in residence at the King's palace. But Mackenzie's gaze was fixed, not on the portraits, but on the two sentries who were both armed with tommy-guns at the end of the corridor, where the big French windows opened out on to the ornamental gardens.

'I'm glad to see you're taking this assassination plot seriously, Colonel,' Mackenzie remarked as Codman opened the door to his own room, which to Mackenzie's eyes seemed like a small palace in itself.

'Yes, I do.' He tapped the breast pocket of his 'Ike' jacket. 'I'm always armed these days and naturally the boss always has his pistols. They're kinda his trade marks. But take a seat, Major.'

Carefully Mackenzie perched himself on the elegant brocaded chair that went with the rococo ceiling and the ormolu clock on the mantelpiece. Codman noticed and grinned. 'Yes, I know, Major. That furniture wasn't designed for our big Anglo-Saxon butts. I'm frightened out of my wits that I break anything. The Italians would be dunning me for money for the rest of my born days, I guess.' His smile vanished. 'So here's the plan.' He glanced at the sheets of paper in front of him on the fancy gilt-rimmed desk. 'Reception for the local worthies at two on the afternoon of Christmas Eve, here. At four they let the kids in for chow – also here. A rest, and I'm sure we'll need it with all of those wop kids. You know how excited they can get.'

Mackenzie nodded, but said nothing.

'Then after our own Christmas Eve dinner and a movie, the boss wants to go to midnight mass with his staff at a quarter to twelve. It'll be a strictly Episcopal service. I quote, "I don't want none of that Papist baloney, Codman. Straight old-time religion."'

Mackenzie nodded again. 'Will it be a service open to all, or just for the general and his staff, Colonel?'

'No, open to anybody who wants to attend. I expect there'll be few Italians, as most of them are Catholic. But it should be packed with our own guys and those of you Britishers who are . . . what do you call 'em . . . Church of England?'

'Yes, Church of England.' Mackenzie pursed his lips and considered for a few minutes, while Codman waited attentively. 'In essence, we've got problems of security with all three events. Both this barn of a palace,' he drew his arm around the huge room, 'and the cathedral are going to be damned difficult to guard. They're both too big and both have several exits and entrances.' He looked directly at the concerned American officer. 'Colonel, is there any way that we can check on the guests here and the worshippers at the midnight mass?'

Codman shook his head. 'No, the boss wouldn't have it. Anyway you can't frisk the local worthies and the kids. As for the guys who'll be attending midnight mass, well you know what those wingdings are like . . .'

Mackenzie didn't. He had long ceased believing in God. Atheism went with the turf. In Intelligence it was wiser not to believe in anything that you couldn't prove.

'Most of them will have sunk a few, probably a lot. It's that typical Christmas Eve thing, Mackenzie. Get a little high and then follow the liquid Christmas spirit with a bit of hymn singing and general uplift.'

Mackenzie forced a laugh. Codman had got it just right. But how in hell's name anyone could believe in the spirit of peace and goodwill to all men in this fourth year of total war was beyond him. 'OK, so what kind of security can the US Army offer us?'

'Not much. Over on the mainland, General Clark is crying out for riflemen, anybody who can hold and fire a Garand. I guess we can raise a company of infantry used for ceremonial duties here, and another company of MPs, if we pull in the guys who direct the traffic from the docks and so on.'

'Pull 'em in, Colonel. We need anybody and everybody.'

Codman made a quick note on the pad in front of him on the spindly eighteenth-century desk. 'Have you any more leads, Mackenzie?'

'Yes and no, Colonel. We're looking for two men, one British and one who we suspect is German. We think the latter is the likely assassin. He's already killed two people.'

Codman was very businesslike. 'Give me his details. We'll have them circulated immediately. The Italian cops aren't much good and I think they're easily bribed as well. But they're not bad at carrying out routine identification checks. I mean, they did that all the time under Musso.'

'Excellent. I'll take care of it at once, Colonel.' He hesitated. 'I—'

'Go on, Mackenzie.'

'Well, Colonel, I don't suppose you could convince General Patton not to attend these Christmas functions – the reception, the midnight mass and the like.'

Codman shook his head almost sorrowfully. 'No, I've seen the general under fire several times here in Sicily already. He's not a man to be easily frightened. In fact, at the front he often took unnecessary risks. No, the boss won't beg off. He'll be there and, you know, Mackenzie,' Codman's voice grew a little wistful, 'I think he'd welcome it if the end came now.' He sighed.

'The boss has just had enough.'

As he left the palazzo, Mackenzie glanced up at the tall French window where he had last seen Patton. The general was still standing there, staring out at nothing. But now he somehow seemed to have shrunk, and his shoulders were bowed in defeat. In a matter of less than an hour, he had

become a silver-haired old man. Abruptly Mackenzie felt
sorry for him. He was like those great military figures of
the past: Wellington, Grant, even Napoleon, who had been
passed over or exiled in some remote forgotten place but
who still waited for the call to arms again, but knowing,
too, that if it didn't come they might as well turn up their
toes and die.

The sight filled him with new resolve. Something had
to be done – and done soon. Patton would, in due course,
receive *his* call, but it wouldn't be much good if he were
dead when it came. He hurried back to his jeep and a waiting
Sergeant Campbell.

'All right, Sergeant!' he snapped, as the NCO started up.
'Let's get the digit out of the orifice. The time has come to
crack this bloody case before the army pensions us off.'

Campbell smiled. 'Righty-ho, sir!' he snapped back with
new enthusiasm. 'Where do we start?'

It was roughly the same question that Chiefie asked himself
as he was thrust forward with the line of walking wounded,
all tagged and exhibiting their bloody bandages with a
hangdog expression as though challenging the sweating
orderlies and nurses *not* to have sympathy with them for
their suffering. There had been a surprisingly large number
of stretcher cases which had had to be taken off first and
carried to the waiting ambulances. For that reason the fat,
bespectacled master sergeant in charge of the operation
had cried at the miserable bunch of walking wounded,
'All right, you guys, form up. We'll walk you to the
hospital.'

That had caused a series of moans, groans and protests
from the wounded, who obviously felt they deserved special
treatment. But the master sergeant had shown no sympathy.
He had shouted, 'Hell, you guys have just enjoyed a sea
voyage in the sunny Mediterranean at the government's

expense. A walk shouldn't worry you. Come on. Get the lead out. Let's go.'

The order had suited Chiefie down to the ground. So far he hadn't been able to steal a blank label or one indicating a suitable illness, such as malaria or jaundice. He didn't want to indicate that he had been wounded. Now he had time while they struggled onwards to see what he could steal that would get him inside the hospital for a while. 'Three squares a day, old lad,' he told himself as he moved forward with the rest of the sorry mob of wounded. 'And a nice cushy ward. Plenty o' time to figure out what to do next.'

But for once the smart little cockney's calculations went askew. For the ticket he stole from the bespectacled GI he found being sick in a urinal once they had entered the great echoing hall of the former Italian hospital wasn't one he would have selected if he had not been in such a hurry. No sooner had he affixed the label to the shabby old naval dungarees he was wearing than he was called to the reception to be confronted by a cropped-haired, middle-aged nurse wearing a similar kind of overall, who checked the label and then snorted, 'Kay, off you go. VD ward first right.'

'VD ward?' he stuttered.

'Yeah, you heard me, sailor. I don't think VD affects your hearing. Now get the hell out of my sight and let me deal with fighting men who have been wounded on a battlefield and not in a frigging cathouse.'

'Oh, my aching back,' Chiefie moaned to himself as he shoved his way to the ward indicated. 'I've landed in the ruddy pox hospital! Now there's gonna be some high jinx.'

There certainly were. While Mackenzie and Campbell 175 launched their new search with renewed energy for the two men missing from the landing barge, the little deserter was subjected to the customary painful and humiliating routine of the VD patient, executed by nurses and attendants who had nothing but contempt for their charges. They felt that VD patients not only wasted precious penicillin that was needed to cure the real wounded, but also that they were no better than the GIs under close guard in the self-inflicted wounds ward. As they sneered at their 'patients', when they injected the new wonder drug as painfully as possible every four hours, 'A shot of this is like gold for the real wounded. I hope it's gonna hurt you, buddy, I honestly do.' And it did.

In Chiefie's case he hadn't got to the cure stage yet. Instead he was being hustled from doctor to doctor, while they attempted to diagnose the exact nature of his 'revolting disease', as one of the medics had contemptuously put it. Bending low, skinny wrinkled rump naked, he was subjected to a rectal examination while an orderly standing ready with a slide in his hand could take a swab of his supposed disease-ridden penis. A catheter was inserted and pulled out slowly, its razor-sharp head scraping away any possible lesions. Thereafter, as the grinning orderly who did the job said scornfully, 'You'll piss blood in six different directions.' And the medic was right.

More than once Chiefie wondered if he had done the right thing by hiding himself away in the pox ward. 'Bloody painful,' he said to himself more than once. 'Not so painful, shipmate, as getting a bullet through yer guts,' he reminded himself. Of course when they discovered he didn't have the clap or syphilis, then there'd be a lot of awkward questions asked. But the way the medics were going at it, it'd be a couple of days before that happened, and by then he'd have an alternative plan worked out.

All the same when he saw the usual morning arrival of the seriously wounded from the mainland front come in to be stripped naked and their bloody bandages ripped off ready for the team of doctors to inspect their wounds, Chiefie had momentary twinges of conscience. He was the long-service regular, a matelot these twenty years or more. They were still kids, wet behind the ears, eighteen and nineteen-year-olds who had probably been in the Kate Karney for nine months or so. Now their lives were ruined. They had lost arms, legs, even eyes. They had no future, but he did as long as he kept dodging the column like this.

The wizened Chiefie wasn't a particularly sensitive man. After all his war years at sea, including being torpedoed twice, he couldn't afford to be. All the same those young men, moaning with pain as the nurses ripped off their bloodstained bandages, moved him. The sight also confused him. It seemed to make his decision about what to do next even more difficult. 'Christ on a crutch,' he moaned to himself. 'What the frig am I gonna do?'

But that was a question that no one save the little deserter could answer.

Five

S tefan waited. He had been brought up in the east, where everything moved half as slow as in the Germany of the Fuhrer's New Order. He was accustomed to waiting.

The city was still quiet. The streets were empty save for a few flea-ridden dogs sniffing the gutters for scraps. But there weren't many of those. Palermo and its ordinary citizens were feeling the pinch. Casually he walked over to the public water tap. Like everything he had seen in this damned country it was still marked with the Roman bundle of sticks, the symbol of the treacherous *fascisti* who had betrayed the Führer and were now fighting on the side of the enemy, the bastards. He turned on the tap. Only a trickle of dark-coloured water came out. Stefan pulled a face. It was typical of these damned macaronis. Nothing worked properly in their damned country. Everything was decayed and useless. Still, he bent and washed his hands and broad Slavic face. He cupped his hands and took a drink of the water. It tasted brackish.

From somewhere there came the delightful smell of real bean coffee being ground to make breakfast. It wasn't the customary ersatz coffee that the macaronis drank – and the SS too for that matter. This was the real thing. He licked his thick, sensual lips. He had plenty of Ami money sewn inside his jacket, nearly a thousand dollars. He could afford to buy anything he liked on the black market. Those Ami dollars had proved very useful since he had fled from the barge and split with Yuri. But he hesitated now. Soon his contact was to appear; he didn't want to miss that meeting. So he went back into the shade and waited.

Now the little square was coming to life slowly. At the cafe attached to the shabby hotel opposite, an elderly unshaven waiter, still in his felt slippers, shuffled out, shouted something to a couple of the mangy dogs that were sniffing around the place, and started to take down the chairs piled up on the tables on the pavement. A couple of workmen, cheap cigarettes glued to their bottom lips, cycled by with bottles of red wine sticking out of the battered attaché cases fixed to their racks. They glanced at the big man lounging in the shadows without interest.

Stefan glanced at his watch. It was about time his contact turned up. Things were beginning to move and he had to be off the street soon. A couple of mules, piled high with vegetables for the Palermo market, ambled up. Behind, a wooden-legged veteran of Mussolini's war clumped along, still dressed in a tattered Italian Army uniform, flicking his stick at the mules' skinny rumps.

Stefan pressed himself deeper into the shadows. Even though the man was a shitty macaroni, he'd still been a soldier, and soldiers were more astute than civilians. Why, the one-legged man might even speak to him in Italian, and his knowledge of that soft, sloppy language – which could not stand a comparison with the hard precision of German, especially the German of the barrack square and fighting front – was limited.

The weary mules, their heads drooping with fatigue and hunger, came level with him, their bells jingling softly. Instinctively Stefan felt for the automatic strapped to his inner right thigh through the hole in his civilian pants.

Now the one-legged veteran came level with Stefan, hidden there in the shadows. Abruptly he stopped. Stefan reached for his automatic. What was the macaroni pig up to?

He hawked and then, turning his head in Stefan's direction, the Sicilian spat a great gob of opaque stuff in the killer's direction. Stefan's face flushed angrily. He was tempted to shoot the man outright. How dare he insult a member of the most elite regiment of the *Waffen* SS. Suddenly, however, the old veteran winked and jerked his thumb over his shoulder in the direction of the shabby house next to the hotel. An instant later he was stomping his way behind his mules again, poking them with his stick and mumbling '*avanti* . . . *avanti*!', leaving Stefan to stare at the figure in the dressing gown who had appeared on the balcony of the house, holding a coffee cup in his hand and apparently savouring the rich aroma of real bean coffee.

For a moment Stefan's mouth dropped open with surprise. It was his contact all right, but he didn't expect *this* particular Italian to be his contact, and placing himself in extreme danger by being so. But there was no time to consider the reasons why he had turned up in Palermo so surprisingly. More and more people were coming into the square. Soon the damned Ami police would be working their usual patrols. He ought to get off the street as soon as possible.

Five minutes later Stefan was seated in the shadow of the roof-top umbrella, surrounded by the usual plant pots and dwarf trees with which the macaronis decorated their balconies and rooftops, savouring the first real coffee he had drunk in years and listening to the man who called himself Joe Victory. But even as he listened, he watched through narrowed eyes the fat American officer with his hanging jowls who had tried to conceal himself in the room beyond the roof garden. The sighting told him two things. One, that it was the fat Ami officer who had brought the wanted Joe Victory over to Sicily at this crucial juncture in the operation; and two, that things were coming to a head if both of them were taking such risks to give him his final briefing. Stefan Hartmann, once of Assault Regiment *Wotan*, told himself the scene was set, the actors were in place. It wouldn't be long before the final act of the drama commenced.

Joe Victory knew that the maid from the hotel had recognized him immediately. She didn't need to scream, even gasp with shock at the sight of him coming down the stairs from the roof garden. She might only have seen him a couple of times. But it was that damned photo they had had taken when he and the boys had been drunk: that one where he'd had his arm around that dope, Giggles. The silly bastard had virtually raped her. For that reason alone she wouldn't forget him. Just like their menfolk, those Sicilian peasant women never forgot *or* forgave. She'd turn him in at the frigging drop of a hat.

For a moment the two of them froze there, her eyes growing ever wider with the shock of seeing him there. Behind Joe Victory the fat Colonel, his briefing finished, came panting down the steep stairs from the roof garden. He stopped abruptly. He took in the scene and realized immediately that something serious had just happened – and he wanted nothing to do with a situation that might compromise him here in Palermo. 'Joe,' he hissed urgently. 'For God's sake do something – *anything*!'

His order awoke Adriana to her danger. She dropped the tin milk jug she was carrying. It rattled to the stone floor. The milk spurted everywhere in the same instant that Joe Victory whipped out his knife.

'Holy Jesus!' the fat colonel gasped. 'No, Joe—'

Too late. The Italian-American lunged forward. His knife flashed in the rays of the early morning sun. The razor-sharp blade ripped the length of the girl's arm. She screamed shrilly. She staggered back. Her arm spurted bright red blood. Joe Victory gasped and lunged again. But despite her terrible pain and fear, she dodged the lunge and turned to run.

159

Joe Victory's dark evil eyes flashed. He couldn't let her escape. Already people were turning to look at the scene alerted by the girl's scream. But they remained frozen where they were. They were all afraid of the Mafia. They knew their own lives would be in danger if they attempted to help her. Adriana knew that too. Dizzy as she now was from loss of blood, she staggered towards the door of the hotel.

Immediately the onlookers parted fearfully, elbowing each other out of the way. They were in the presence of death. They were taking no chances. Joe Victory didn't even notice, he was so confident of the power of the Mafia over these stupid peasants. He brushed them to one side, knife clasped close to his side, almost hidden like a dentist hides his forceps as he approaches a fearful patient about to have his tooth extracted.

Her eyes liquid and wide with pain, Adriana backed off, holding her bleeding arm with the other in a desperate attempt to stop the blood flow. She knew she could expect no help from the crowd. Like all Sicilians they were deadly afraid of Mafia revenge. Her only hope would be from the two Englishmen.

She screamed in the same moment she stumbled over the basket of potatoes that one of the stall holders had dropped in his panic. She attempted to steady herself, to no avail. The loss of blood had made her feel dizzy already. Joe Victory saw his chance. He lunged. His knife slid up to the hilt in her stomach. She screamed again piteously. The mafioso showed no mercy. His dark, pock-marked face contorted with hate and the lust of killing. He ripped the sharp blade upwards, tearing open the wall of her stomach mercilessly. He felt the hand holding his knife flush hot with her blood.

Hastily he drew the bloodstained knife out with a dreadful sucking noise. '*Putana*!' he cursed and thrust home the blade yet once more. '*Die!*'

160

This time she did not scream. Instead a low moan escaped from her gaping mouth. Her legs started to crumple beneath her, as the whites of her eyes turned upwards. She was dying. He knew the signs. He had been present at enough Mafia murders to know. Now she was remaining upright only because he was holding her like that with his knife.

'For Chrissake, Joe,' the fat colonel on the stairs cried frantically. 'Let's get the hell out of here, man!'

Joe Victory shook his head like a man trying to wake up from some terrible nightmare. Suddenly he realized his own danger. The American military police patrol could appear any moment. He withdrew the knife. She gave a sad little moan – more of a sigh really. Slowly she started to slide down the wall, trailing blood along it. Hastily he wiped the blade clean on her blouse. Then he turned and was pushing his way through the silent, awed crowd, watching the dying girl as she slumped to the ground among the potatoes, her head askew, her bosom rising and falling ever slower as the spirit fled her tortured body.

The scream wakened Mackenzie from his dream. Reluctantly. They had made love twice. They had done so with a silent kind of passion. It was understandable. Neither spoke the other's language well enough for eloquent words of love. He had slid himself into the hot wet nothingness of her beautiful young body. She gasped, as if he were hurting her. Like a frisky young mare she had bucked and heaved so much that he had half imagined that she was trying to escape him. But he had been wrong. She had been crazy, even frenzied with passion.

Afterwards she had lain in his arms. He had still been able to feel her heart beating frantically with the excitement of it all. With a slightly shaking hand he had stroked her damp hair gently, trying to soothe her. Then he had wished he had known enough Italian to say something of importance to her, but what that importance was, he had not rightly known. So they had lain in each other's arms, happy, silent and oblivious – or so it seemed – to their future in this crazy world at war.

Now that scream, coming from so very far away, broke his dream and he was suddenly back in 1943. Instinctively he reached for his .38 hanging in its holster from his bedstead. That shrill scream heralded trouble, he knew that already.

Campbell was quicker off the mark. These days he kept out of Mackenzie's way till duty time. He didn't want to get in the way of the major's affair with the chamber maid. Mackenzie deserved *some* pleasure, even though it might be just a quick fling in bed. Now dressed and armed, Campbell pelted down the steps of the hotel, bursting out into the open. A dark-haired runt of an Italian in a flashy suit was running away, barging people to one side in his haste. Later Campbell 175 also thought he caught a glimpse of an American soldier. Now, however, as he pushed his way into the crowd himself, revolver already drawn but unable to shoot for fear of hitting one of the civilians, his attention was forcefully distracted from the running man. For it was then he spotted the girl Adriana hunched against the wall, her front smeared with bright red blood, her head lolling to one side. '*Ach du Scheisse!*' he cried in his native language, shocked beyond all measure by that terrible sight, for he knew even then that the girl was dying.

'Get the hell out of my way!' he shouted in Italian, face purple with sudden fury. He bent and raised her head tenderly. She was still breathing, just. His eyes took in the terrible wound in her stomach from which her intestines were beginning to slide like a silent grey-pink serpent. He fumbled in his trouser pocket for his shell dressing. But even as he brought out the wadded bandage he knew that it was useless. The wound was too grave and the bleeding too profuse to be stopped by the infantryman's simple bandage. *'Mi vuol chiamare un dottore!'* he called over his shoulder as he attempted to push back the girl's protruding gut. When not one of the gaping onlookers staring at the dying girl with morbid fascination moved, he bellowed angrily, *'Dottore pronto . . . ambulatorio medico!'*

It was while he was doing this, uselessly trying to keep the girl alive till a doctor arrived, that Mackenzie encountered him. He skidded to a stop. *'Adriana!'* he gasped, his voice suddenly choked.

Campbell 175 looked up. 'I've sent for a doctor, sir.' He shook his head. 'But . . .' his voice faded away. He could say no more.

Mackenzie knelt next to the dying girl. 'Adriana,' he asked foolishly, *'le fa male?'*

Her eyes flickered open at the sound of his voice. *'Tanto,'* she breathed weakly.

'A doctor is coming,' he tried to reassure her. 'Soon.' But in these last terrible years of war Mackenzie had seen so many people die; he knew there was no hope for her. The most skilled doctor, even if he arrived that moment, couldn't save her. She was dying by the second. He took her hand, but she drew away. Strange mumbling sounds were coming from her mouth. He bent forward to catch them, they were so faint and confused. Her hand reached out. Trailing her forefinger through her own blood she appeared to be scribbling something on the pavement. 'Don't move, darling,' he urged, his own face contorted with pain and sorrow at the young girl's suffering. *'Please.'*

She didn't appear to hear. With the last of her strength, she continued the crazy scrawl with her own blood as the howl of a siren further down one of the streets off the square indicated that an ambulance was on its way. Mackenzie shot a glance in that direction, willing the ambulance to arrive and help her before it was too late.

But it was already too late.

When Mackenzie turned back to her, he gasped with shock. Her hand was sprawled out in the pool of her own blood, the fingers still. 'Adriana!' he cried, and then his voice broke helplessly and he could say no more.

Behind, Campbell stared at the red smear and what she had tried to write in her blood. 'V . . . I . . . C . . . T . . .' the four letters were sufficient. 'Victory,' he said grimly to himself. She'd recognized her murderer all right.

He had been that Mafia thug known as Joe Victory!

Six

The fat colonel from Clark's HQ at Caserta looked ill at ease to Codman, as he waited to see Patton. His hanging jowls were flushed and there was a thin line of perspiration above his upper lip. Obviously something was troubling him and Codman hoped it was a nice juicy problem. For he remembered the fat colonel's insulting behaviour to the boss at the dinner in Caserta. Then he thought again. Was the fat colonel bringing further bad news for General Patton and was now worried about the latter's reaction? Everyone in the army knew just how hair-trigger Ole Blood an' Guts' temper was.

Codman had offered the vistor one martini and he had drained the cocktail in one gulp, as if he had real need of it. Now Codman offered him another one from the shaker. Perhaps a second cocktail might loosen the fat colonel up a little and he'd find out why Clark had sent him to see Patton like that.

The colonel, who was supposedly a personal aide to General Clark, as was Codman to Patton, didn't hesitate, though Codman wouldn't have even dreamed of taking a drink when he was doing military business with the boss.

'Sure,' the fat colonel answered as Codman agitated the shaker. 'I could do with another drink. As long as you can give me a peppermint to suck before the meeting.'

Codman gave him a fake smile. 'All taken care of, Colonel,' he replied and neatly poured out the martini, deftly adding an olive. 'But tell me, if you can, why did General Clark send you here, just before Christmas like this? Is it something very important?'

The drink seemed to have steadied the other man's nerve somewhat, for he said, with a sudden smirk on his fat face, 'Wish I could, Colonel. But what I've got to say is strictly for General Patton's ears only. You know your general has caused a lot of trouble of late. In the States that newspaper buzzard, Drew Pearson, is giving him a real roasting in his syndicated column. And there are others too. General Clark thinks it wiser to keep this piece of information strictly on a one-to-one basis. The fewer people in the know, the better.'

Codman felt himself flushing angrily. The fat bastard was implying that he might betray whatever this thing was to the press. Didn't he know that he, Charley Codman, would die for the general if needs be? But being the conservative Bostonian that he was, he kept his temper and said coldly, 'I see.' But Codman could tell from the smirk which now appeared on the fat colonel's face that whatever the latter had to say to General Patton, it was going to be unpleasant. So now he restricted himself to making small talk until the general made his appearance.

Patton did so, a few minutes later. Although he was as smartly dressed as usual, all gleaming brass, creased pants and naturally his twin pistols – though the combat zone was miles away on the mainland now – his normally erect shoulders were bowed and his hair seemed to Codman whiter and thinner than ever. 'Good morning, gentlemen,' he said and casually acknowledged their salutes before sitting down on the spindly chair, as if he were unutterably weary.

'Colonel Hermann, sir,' the fat colonel introduced himself. 'Personal aide to General Clark, sir.'

Patton nodded, but said nothing, which was unusual for Ole Blood an' Guts.

'Sir,' Hermann continued, flashing a glance at Codman, 'I have been instructed by General Clark to convey an important piece of news to you personally . . . and the news is intended for your ears only. Perhaps Colonel Codman might be asked to step outside for a few moments, sir?'

Patton seemed to come to life again. 'Colonel Codman will *not* step outside, as you put it, Hermann,' he snapped swiftly. 'I trust Charley Codman as I would trust my own son. He stays.' He whipped out one of the big cigars and lit it slowly, fussing over the end, taking pleasure in seeing Hermann squirm as he debated with himself what he should do. Finally he was finished with the cigar and, taking it out of his mouth, he added, 'Well, Hermann, let's piss or get off the pot. I haven't got all the time in the world.'

At that moment Codman admired his boss more than he had ever done before. He had faced down the fat colonel, although he knew that whatever the news he had brought from Clark wasn't going to be good for him.

'Yessir,' Hermann said. He was sweating again. 'Well, sir. Yesterday General Clark received a top secret message from General Eisenhower, the Supreme—'

'Goddamit, Hermann, I know who Ike is!' Patton interrupted him angrily. 'Get on with it.'

Now Codman allowed himself a grin. The boss was back on his old form and he was highly pleased that this fat Colonel Hermann was at the receiving end of the boss's anger.

'Sir, if you think it's all right, this is it. Two things.' Hermann cleared his throat in his self-important manner. 'You are not to command the Seventh Army's invasion of southern France.'

Codman winced. The boss had been pinning his hopes that, after this long exile in Sicily after the summer's slapping incident, he might be given back the command of his old army for that attack on southern France which was to link up with the main invasion in northern France. This was a body blow and both he and Hermann could see by the look on Patton's face that it hurt damnably.

But Hermann wasn't finished yet. 'There's another thing, sir,' he said. 'General Clark thought it might interest you.'

'What is it?' Patton asked tonelessly.

'He has heard from the Supreme Commander that General Bradley is scheduled to command all US ground troops in Great Britain ready for the invasion.'

'The tentmaker!' Patton groaned. 'The tentmaker is going to command a US Army!'

Codman's heart sank. General Omar Bradley, maliciously nicknamed the 'tentmaker' by the boss due to his unusual Arabic first name, had once been Patton's subordinate in the Battle of Sicily. He had been a subordinate of whom the boss didn't think much. Once Patton had told Codman: 'Charley, Bradley is a man of great mediocrity. He has, however, many attributes which are considered desirable in a general. He wears glasses, has a strong jaw and talks profoundly about nothing.' He chuckled and had added, 'His success is due to a lack of backbone.' Now the tentmaker was to take command of the invasion army, a command that Patton had once sworn: 'I'd rightly give my left ball, Charley, to get that frigging job.'

It was the final body blow and Codman saw how the boss seemed to almost crumple, face suddenly ashen. For a moment his loyal aide thought that Patton was going to suffer a heart attack, the shock was so great. But he pulled himself together and said quietly, 'Thank you for the information, Hermann. Give my best regards to your General Clark. Colonel Codman here will see you get a lunch before you fly back to Caserta.'

As Hermann came to attention, his fat jowls wobbling with the effort, he asked, 'Will you be attending? The lunch, sir, I mean.'

Patton shook his head. Quietly he said, 'No, I don't feel very hungry, Hermann. Goodbye.'

'Goodbye, sir,' Hermann replied smartly, a look of triumph on his face as the general went out slowly. Codman's heart went out to the boss. The news had almost broken him. For months since he had been relieved of his command he had been whistling in the wind, hoping that something would come along and he'd receive an active command once more. Now it seemed that Hermann, as his rival's emissary, had dashed his hopes for good. There was no more fighting for the poor old warhorse. Now it would be back to the States in due course and a slippered retirement for the boss, somewhere warm where he'd drink too much and probably be dead within the year.

Colonel Hermann waited till Patton had disappeared before saying, 'I'll take a rain check on that lunch, Codman, if it's okay with you.'

Codman nodded.

'I thought while I'm here I ought to see the sights. There's nothing much going on back at HQ, what with Christmas coming up and everything. The general's too busy with the HQ party and all that kind of stuff.' He picked up his helmet liner from the fragile little eighteenth-century table and plonked it on his shaven skull. 'And when I've seen the sights, Codman, I might go and get laid.' He winked. 'They tell me these Sicilian dames are real hot potatoes. So long.' And with that he was gone, waddling out into the thin winter sunlight and leaving Codman angry and puzzled. Colonel Hermann had really done a job on the boss and he could guess why. His chief, General Clark, had been eager to rub Patton up the wrong way, turn the knife in the wound. But why was Hermann wanting to stay over and see the 'sights'? To Codman's way of thinking, Colonel Joseph S. Hermann, Jnr was the last person in the world who would be interested in Sicilian antiquities.

Colonel Codman was not the only person puzzled a little by Colonel Hermann's activities in Sicily. Sergeant Campbell 175 was too. For the time being he had left Major Mackenzie to see what could be done about the poor dead maid, Adriana, and her piss-poor family somewhere out in the countryside. He was to concern himself with Joe Victory with the utmost urgency, and with Mackenzie's threat ringing in his ears – 'Don't let me get my hands on the murderous bastard, or he won't live to go on trial, Sergeant' – he did just that.

He'd already come to the conclusion that Joe Victory had returned to the island with the aid of the unknown American that had been spotted at the scene of the crime. Ever since the business with the landing barge, the US Navy had tightened up its security net around Sicily. There'd be no more smuggling of persons or black market goods on to the island from the mainland. So there was only one way that Joe Victory could have re-entered the island, and that was by air, but the air routes were controlled by the Yanks one hundred per cent.

It hadn't taken Campbell long to find out how many machines had flown into the two fields of Palermo and Messina in the last week. Hurriedly he had gone through the lists of military passengers *and* the aircrews who had flown the planes – he was leaving nothing to chance. But there had been no sign of any Italian flying with these Yanks into Sicily until he had come to what the Americans were now calling 'VIP flights', a new abbreviation for 'Very Important Persons'. Here an excited Campbell 175 had discovered that a VIP flight from Caserta to Palermo had transported a certain Colonel Hermann, and this staff officer, whoever he was, had brought with him his 'official Italian interpreter'.

There had been no name attached to this Italian. There had been a clue, however, to indicate that he wasn't a Yank. It was the usual military designation after the 'official Italian

170

interpreter'. That had read, 'Civ. AMGOT', which translated as 'Civilian, American Military Government'. And the smart little German Jew knew he didn't need a crystal ball to guess that a civilian working for the American Military Government in the Naples area was more than likely to be a member of the Mafia. Could this apparent mafioso be Joe Victory?

'Follow it up, Campbell,' Mackenzie had ordered urgently over the phone when Campbell had reported his suspicions to the major. 'It's the only lead we've got. Perhaps now we're finally getting towards some solution to this bloody awful mess. And don't be scared of treading on the Yanks' toes.'

'No sir, I won't.'

But Sergeant Campbell wouldn't need to step on the Yanks' toes – at least not yet. For help from an unexpected quarter was on its way. The little petty officer born within the sound of Bow bells had made his decision. He was going to hide no longer. He was coming out, cost whatever it may.

Seven

C hiefie had known he was being a bleeding fool, but that morning when they brought survivors into the American hospital, he had been simply unable to stop himself. They were British, the first British apart from himself that the Yank medics had seen, and they were matelots as well. Their ship had been torpedoed by a German sub off Bari and they had been rescued by the US Navy and brought to Palermo instead of to the British Army hospital at Bari.

Now the fortunate few who had survived, black-faced in their oil-soaked dungarees and overalls, were being helped inside or carried in on stretchers to where the American doctors and nurses were waiting to take charge of them. Some had lacerated faces and skulls, bright red against the slimy oily blackness. Others, probably from the engine room of the torpedoed ship, had been scalded gruesomely by the rush of escaping steam. Their eyebrows and eyelashes had gone and, in one case, their ears.

Now those who could still stand, shivering and shocked as they were, looked in silent wonder at the immaculate whiteness of the hospital and the sight of the Yank nurses in their khaki uniforms, while others crouched against the walls, smearing them with an oily blackness, coughing and vomiting violently, a watery mixture of sea and oil, their shoulders shaking like little kids sobbing their hearts out.

Chiefie swallowed hard. Apart from a couple of petty

172

officers like himself, the British sailors were mere kids – 'hostilities only' lads – who had probably never even seen the sea before they had joined the Royal Navy. Now these kids, still wet behind the ears, had seen their ships sunk beneath them and suffered the loss of their comrades, drowning helplessly in a sea of escaping oil. Chiefie's heart went out to them. 'Poor young sods. Just off their mothers' titties and now this. What a frigging world!'

A nurse turned. 'Enough of that filth, soldier,' she snapped, as she started to unwind a black bandage off one of the survivors, the kid crying with the pain of flesh ripping away with the cotton. Then she recognized him. 'Off you go back to the clap cases,' she added with a sneer. 'We don't want your kind here, mixing with these brave young guys.'

Old Chiefie felt as if someone had just stuck a sharp knife into his guts. He reeled back and momentarily held on to the wall for support. The hot-tempered retort he had prepared for the nurse died on his lips. She was right. What use was he? He was just a bloody malingerer, a bleeding lead-swinger. He pulled himself together. Slowly and thoughtfully he walked away leaving the kids to their agony and suffering, closing his ears to the cries of pain and vomiting.

It was at that moment he made his decision. He knew he couldn't dodge the column any longer. He had taken King George's shilling over twenty years before and now he had to repay that debt, cost what it may – and somehow he knew it was going to cost him plenty.

That afternoon he had packed his few bits and pieces and reported to the hospital's admin wing. He knew, of course, he could have walked out of the place and no one would have stopped him. But then he would have been back on the streets, trying to find some Eyetie tart so that he could get his feet under the table till he could start operating on the black market once more. But that was not what he wanted. He wanted to clean the slate and get back into the war sooner rather than later, once they'd let him out of the glasshouse.

The bespectacled admin lieutenant was caught completely off guard by Chiefie's confession. 'You mean . . .' he stuttered, peering at Chiefie through his steel-rimmed GI glasses as if he were a creature from another world, 'you haven't got the clap . . . and . . . you're a deserter . . . gone over the hill?'

'Yessir,' Chiefie had answered, not one bit concerned by the lieutenant's reaction; his mind on other things that were soon to come. Dimly he heard the screams of the British survivors as they now started to inject massive doses of anti-tetanic serum into those who had suffered serious wounds or second-degree burns. 'If there's a British unit on the island, I'd like to surrender myself to them. I'd like to get it over with as soon as possible. Besides, I might have some intelligence for your own people, which could be of some use.'

The officer wasn't listening. If the Britisher wanted to surrender to his own people, he'd be only too happy to oblige. He'd got enough admin problems on his hands already. Besides he had a hot date with a nubile *signora* tonight and he wanted to be off early, armed with his carton of Luckies and a wad of rubbers. 'Can do,' he said. 'Now wait outside, sailor, and we'll fetch the boys in blue.'

Half an hour later, after the lieutenant had made a few phone calls to Patton's palazzo, the 'boys in blue', in the form of two gigantic US military policeman, had duly delivered Chiefie to a surprised Campbell 175 in an office, given to him by Codman, in the palazzo HQ.

He stared at the wizened deserter and told himself he was a real old salt, who wouldn't have given himself up so tamely like this if he didn't want something in return. To Campbell's surprise, Chiefie didn't haggle or bargain. Instead he said,

'Sarge, I'm prepared to do my time if necessary, though I do hear that the old country's so short of fighting men that the authorities are prepared to waive a sentence if a matelot is prepared to go back to the firing line, which I am.' Chiefie didn't pause to see what Campbell's reaction, if any, was. Instead he continued right on with, 'Now, I can see from your cap badge, Sarge, that you belong to the Intelligence Corps.'

'Something like that,' Campbell 175 answered in a non-committal manner.

'Well, you're the bloke for me, Sarge. Cos I think I've got some information for you.'

'What kind of info?'

'This.' Chiefie drew a deep breath and plunged in, knowing that if he fell into the hands of the Eyetie thugs now, they'd probably slit his gizzard without a second thought. 'I was the skipper of that barge off Palermo which you've probably found by now. You know, the one that had the nasty to do with the Yank patrol boat.'

Campbell 175 sat up abruptly. This was it. 'Tell me more!' he exclaimed excitedly.

Hurriedly Chiefie told him what had happened and how the two supposed Italians with the yellow hair had killed his crew while he'd made a run for it and had managed to escape. 'It was nip and tuck, Sarge, but I made it and went to ground in the pox hospital.'

Campbell smiled. 'We never thought of that, Chief Petty Officer. Very smart of you. Now, can you tell me more about the chaps with the yellow hair?'

Chiefie did so, pointing out that he didn't think they were Eyeties because between themselves they had spoken 'another lingo that wasn't Eyetie, Sarge'.

'You're right, Chiefie,' Campbell agreed. 'They were SS men.' He allowed the old sailor a little bit of information, but he didn't tell him that there was only one of the 'yellow-haired chaps' still among the land of the living.

Chiefie whistled through his front teeth. 'Cor ferk a duck, Sarge! SS men, eh. But what were SS men doing with that Mafia arsehole Joe Victory and that Yankee boss of his?'

'What did you say?'

Chiefie repeated his statement.

At that moment Campbell 175 could have whistled through his teeth himself, he was that surprised by the other man's revelation; but he had never mastered that particular art as a boy. So he contented himself with asking, trying at the same time to contain his mounting excitement, 'Can you tell me any more about this American?'

'Not that much, Sarge. The Yank tried to keep in the background. After all, he'd be a bloody fool to be seen consorting with that dago thug, Joe Victory. But old Chiefie caught 'em together when they didn't know I was around. First off, the Yank was an officer. One time I saw him from a distance at the docks in Reggio and I could see the stuff on his shoulders glinting in the sunshine and the Yanks who were passing were saluting him. An' yer know, Sarge, the Yanks are dead sloppy when it comes to saluting yer officers and gents. So my guess was that he was a high-ranking one.' He nodded his head vigorously, as if confirming his own statement.

'Go on,' Campbell 175 urged.

'There ain't much more, Sarge . . . Oh yes, he was fat, the Yank officer, and he was obviously into the rackets with Joe Victory, cos we – me and the poor lads – took some stuff across from the mainland to here that was obvious Yankee stuff.' The little deserter paused momentarily before continuing. 'But that last time the Yank had more on his mind than us peddling a bit of black market petrol and drugs.'

'Drugs?'

Chiefie explained about the white packet and added, 'But

176

to my way of thinking, Sarge, them drugs were handed over
to Joe Victory as a kind of payment for getting them yeller
buggers across. Yer, I'm sure. Them two were not taking
their orders from Joe Victory.'

'You mean, they were acting on orders from this fat
high-ranking American officer?'

'Dead sure, Sarge.'

Campbell 175's mind raced. They were on to something
tangible at last, he told himself, but how did it all add up,
for Chrissake?

Campbell explained to a grave-faced Major Mackenzie
half an hour later, while a now relaxed Chiefie puffed a big
American cigar outside, still under the guard of the giant
US military policemen. 'We've got this thug Joe Victory
mixed up in this dirty business, we've got the blond-haired
killer who belongs to the SS, and a mysterious American
officer who is apparently doing more than just indulging in
the black market racketeering that most of these fat bastards
are involved in. But why, sir,' he posed the overwhelming
question,' should an American colonel want to kill an
American general, namely our limey-hating Blood an' Guts
Patton?'

Mackenzie, still dust-begrimed and weary from his jour-
ney up into the mountains to meet Adriana's humble peasant
parents, did not answer immediately. He was still preoccupied with that meeting.

The whole family had met him as he had bumped his
way up the rough hill track to the collection of tumbledown
houses which made up the village at the top. There was the
granny, her toothless face withered and terribly wrinkled so
she almost looked like a mummy's skull. Endless sun and
back-breaking labour in their pathetic little fields had done
that to her. The mother, surrounded by yet more children,
was fat and her bare legs were a mass of red and black
varicose veins due to child-bearing. The father was small

and yellow-toothed, holding his arms protectively around the family's one possession as if he were prepared to die for it: a bundle of ragged hide and skinny ribs which turned out to be a little donkey. They, and all the villagers he had met were like that. Ragged, lousy, poor scarecrows, riddled with disease and lice, starved, with angular bones and stringy, dull white flesh showing through the tears in the rags they wore.

He had not known what to say to them. His Italian they barely understood anyway, and he suspected they spoke some obscure Sicilian dialect among themselves. '*Io non parlo siciliano*,' he had said before unloading the tins of meat, coffee, packets of pasta and the like that he had brought and solemnly handing them to the two uncomprehending women, the granny and Adriana's swollen mother, repeating '*ecco*' time and time again to encourage them to take the goods. Even the children seemed scared or reluctant to accept the Hershey bars he had brought from the American HQ, looking at them as if they had never seen chocolate in all their lifetime. Perhaps they hadn't.

Then he had told them his news.

He had been prepared for an outburst of grief. But he had not anticipated such a massive outpouring of emotion. The women threw their black aprons over their hysterically distorted faces. The children burst out crying, wringing their hands in abject misery as the tears rolled down their cheeks, while the old man who had been Adriana's father stroked the donkey's head gently, mouth open and gasping, as if he were choking to death.

Mackenzie had not been able to stand it any longer. He had gone back to the jeep in silence and without a word of goodbye. He started the little vehicle as quietly as he could, because he didn't want to disturb them in their grief, and had rolled back down the bumpy hill track. Behind him they continued to wail and sob in a world that was as different from his as the moon is from the sun. But when he had reached the road once more he had opened up, racing the jeep all out, his sorrow replaced by a mood of burning anger and a fervent desire for revenge.

Now as he faced Campbell 175 he pondered the question that the NCO had just posed him until finally he answered, his voice and emotions under control once more – indeed he felt a new iciness in his blood that made him unable to feel passion any more. 'I don't know, Campbell. But I intend to find out – *soon*. Now do this for me, please. Get down to the reception, chase that Eyetie out of his office and contact Colonel Codman by phone. He's a good man. He'll cooperate.'

'Sir?'

'Tell him what we now know. Tell him, too, that this matter is highly confidential and that we suggest he keep it under his hat, not even telling General Patton about this American officer working with the Mafia and apparently intent on assassinating his master.'

'Sir?'

'Then ask him this. Does he know of any Yank officer – perhaps a major or field grade rank – who has recently flown into Sicily, perhaps in the company of an Italian civilian. If he does, have the man placed under close arrest at once. If he doesn't, ensure that all American flights back to mainland Italy are cancelled. There can't be many of them at this time of the year, just before Christmas.'

'Will do, sir!' Campbell answered smartly, reaching for his forage cap. 'And then, sir?' he asked as he reached the door and saluted.

'What then?' Mackenzie echoed grimly. 'We get our paws on the murdering Yank bastard and grill him till we get the truth out of him.'

'The Yank authorities won't like that, sir,' Campbell objected, though inwardly he was already savouring the thought of roughing up Joe Victory's probable accomplice, and then some.

'The Yanks won't know. And if they do, so what?' Mackenzie shrugged carelessly. 'The gloves are off now, Campbell. All right, get on your bike.'

Campbell allowed himself a little smile. 'I'm on my way already, sir.' As he hurried down the corridor outside, he started to whistle almost happily . . .

Eight

The fat colonel hit the jeep's brakes hard. The jeep skidded and shuddered to a violent stop. '*Porco di Madonna!*' Joe Victory cursed as his head slammed against the windscreen. 'What the hell—'

'Shut yer dago mouth!' the fat colonel cut him off sharply. He swung the steering wheel to the right, leaving the road and heading for an olive grove. Satisfied that they couldn't be seen from the road, he heaved his bulk from the seat and went to the edge of the ancient stunted trees, while Joe Victory stared at the back of his now sweat-blackened olive shirt, thinking the *Americano* had suddenly gone crazy.

But Colonel Hermann was anything but crazy. Now he was totally preoccupied with saving his fat hide. For up ahead, he could see that there were extra guards on the gate of Palermo's Army Air Corps field and, what was more significant, other guards around the C-47 which was due to take him back to Caserta, leaving Joe Victory and his thugs to carry out the job – 'make their bones' as he knew the mafiosi called it – while he was in the clear at Caserta HQ.

Joe Victory joined him, still nursing his head. Crouching beside the colonel, who was breathing heavily now, and sensing the American's fear, he asked, 'What's the deal?'

'The deal is this. I'm not going back to Caserta today, and neither are you.'

'What d'ya mean?'

'What I said. There's something going on over there at the field and I want no part in it.'

Now it was Joe Victory's turn to be afraid. Like the colonel he, too, was very concerned with his own precious skin. 'You mean they're wise to us?'

'I don't know. But I'm not taking that chance, especially as you're with me. I mean, if they start making real enquiries they'll soon wise up to the fact that you aren't authorized to fly with me in an American Air Corps plane. You're a liability at this moment, Joe.'

The Mafia man didn't question the 'liability' business; indeed he didn't want to know why the colonel considered him such a burden. In Mafia circles, 'liabilities' were soon disposed of – in concrete coffins and the like. Instead he whined, 'What we gonna do, Colonel?'

'This. We're gonna get our butts back to that jeep and make it to Palermo. There we're going to lie low till you-know-what's over.' Suddenly an idea came to him and the worried look vanished from his fat face. 'Indeed, I'm going to go to midnight mass in the cathedral tomorrow night.'

Joe Victory looked at his companion as if he had suddenly gone mad. 'Midnight mass?' he breathed. 'What the hell d'you wanna do that for? You ain't even no Catholic!'

But as always Colonel Hermann was keeping his secrets to himself. He and his kind had always worked – and survived – on that basis . . .

Back in the late summer of 1942 when Boss Krause had learned of the US military's plans in Europe, he had called them together, told them that 'if any of you men breathe even a word of what I'm gonna propose now to anybody else, well . . .' He had drawn the cheap cigar which he chewed all the time from between his loose, wet lips and pointed it at the group of party bosses as if it were a lethal weapon, and breathed, 'you might not be around to see 1943. Kay?'

182

They had nodded solemnly. They were all well-fed middle-aged men who controlled their little political empires in virtually every state of the union; important men who could make or break others, but they were all afraid of Boss Krause sitting there in his rocking chair, cuspidor between his legs, his braces dangling and his grubby shirt open so that they could see his fat gut covered by grizzled old man's hair.

'I don't need to tell you fellahs,' he continued in the hick accent he affected which appealed to his own voters back home, though indeed he was Harvard educated and had once been a member of the Supreme Court in his home state. 'The party's priority is to get that goddam kike out of the White House and end this New Deal shit that's ruining the country.'

Again they had nodded dutifully, not one bit surprised that Boss Krause addressed President Roosevelt as that 'goddam kike', for they knew that the fat old schemer, moving his cheap cigar from one end of his mouth to the other, hated 'kikes', 'wops', 'micks', 'niggers', but most of all, Roosevelt's democrats. He did it for a good reason. *Money!* He took money, lots of it, from rail, coal, steel, oil, to maintain those politicians in power who wouldn't – and couldn't – injure their interests. And his listeners knew that since America had entered the war and industry was making huge profits, industry's bigger threat came from Roosevelt's young pink New Dealers who might cut those excessive profits.

'Kay,' Boss Krause had continued after spitting noisily into the jug-shaped cuspidor at his feet. It was another of his 'good ole boy' acts that matched his dangling red suspenders. 'Now we all know that Jewboy Roosevelt is going to run for re-election in '44. A cripple like that . . .' He had shaken his head as if he could no longer understand the world. 'And there's nobody at the moment who can beat him.' He paused and raised his dirty right finger like

183

an old-time preacher going to give his congregation some fire and brimstone. 'But there may be by the end of next year, 1943. Someone waiting in the wings, like Grant waited to be called to fame – and the presidency.'

It was then that Boss Krause had outlined his dramatic plan. To any but these shady ward bosses and Tammany Hall politicians it would have sounded crazy, suggesting three unknown colonels, two of them due for retirement soon, to be capable of challenging President Roosevelt and entering the White House in due course. But these were men who were used to working in smoke-filled dingy backrooms of saloons and the like, using money, threats, promises to make the most unlikely of projects come through. So they listened attentively to the fat old political boss as he revealed the names of the three men who he thought might succeed.

'There's Brigadier Eisenhower in England. He's been joined there by another newly appointed brigadier general, Wayne Clark. And finally there's a crazy jerk, who you might already have heard of, that crackpot Brigadier General – or maybe he's Major General by now – George Patton.' He hawked and spat another gob of phlegm into the spitoon. 'Crazy as a loon he might be, that Patton guy, but he's got style and, like the other two, he's going somewhere *and* he is one of us. Gentlemen,' Boss Krause had concluded, 'I give you our next candidate for the '44 election: *George S. Patton!*'

But the events of spring and summer 1943 had torpedoed the old kingmaker's plans to a great extent. As Boss Krause had predicted, all three of the potential presidency candidates had done well and made a name for themselves on the battlefields of Europe, especially Patton. He had taken over the defeated US Second Corps in North Africa after Rommel had trounced it at the Kasserine Pass in February 1943, and had led it to victory. Given command of the new US Seventh Army in the summer of that year, Patton had fought a quick battle in Sicily and in thirty short days had cleared the enemy out of the island. Then had come the slapping incident.

'Patton's blotted his damned copybook,' Boss Krause had snorted. 'Well and truly. The press hounds and the bleeding hearts are going to hound him into the ground. Forget Patton. He's history now.'

Then they had concentrated their attention on Clark, the commander of the Fifth Army. 'He's one of us,' Boss Krause had stated. 'He's ruthless when the occasion demands. He's vain and he wants to end this war – which he's winning – a big shot. He's our man and you, Hermann, are going to be our man at his HQ. You are going to guide Clark and see he's not gonna fuck up like Patton has done.'

Hermann, a pre-war major in his state's National Guard division, had enjoyed his fall at Clark's HQ. Promoted colonel and an aide to Clark, it has been an easy life. There had been the dames, young enough to be his daughters; the black market, which had made him several thousand greenbacks already; and the Mafia, who could carry out the unpleasant little jobs with which he didn't want to soil his own hands, for him. Yes, all in all his three months at Clark's HQ at Caserta had been some of the most pleasant of his life since he had been a backstreet lawyer in the days of Prohibition when he had enjoyed more dames than he could handle and had gambled away thousands of dollars of illegal dough every month at the bookies.

Then had come the signal from Eisenhower's HQ in London. Their man there had passed on the bad news that Patton was going to be rehabilitated in the new year. He was going to be given a command in the coming invasion of Europe, the Third US Army probably.

In the States Boss Krause had hit the roof. 'Jesus H!' he had cried over the scrambler phone when Hermann had told him. 'That jerk Patton'll go all out to upstage Clark. You wait and see. They hate each other's guts as it is. Patton'll go through hell and high water to achieve some kind of glory out there in France and that weak sister Eisenhower won't be able to stop him. Our man Clark will be left commanding his forgotten army in Italy, while Patton's making the headlines in France – even if he's got to get his whole goddam army killed in the process!'

Hesitantly, already seeing his comfortable existence in Caserta beginning to crumble, Hermann had asked, 'What am I supposed to do, Boss?'

Boss Krause hadn't wasted any words. He had snarled down the phone, '*Kill Patton!*'

Now as the colonel and Joe Victory prepared to drive back to Palermo, it occurred to the former that he hadn't seen the yellow-haired hitman since his companion had killed the girl. 'Say,' he asked, 'where's that guy you had sent here to do the job?'

Joe Victory shrugged carelessly, his mind on more important things. 'I don't know.'

'What the Sam Hill d'ya mean, you don't know?' Hermann snorted.

'What I say?'

'Sweet Jesus,' Hermann cursed and then fell silent. But when they were back in the jeep and he had taken over the wheel again, he said, completely without emotion, 'OK big shot, *you're gonna kill Patton now!*'

Nine

J ust after four that morning Stefan woke. As always he
was fully awake at once. His years in SS Assault Regiment *Wotan* had taught him the value of being immediately
alert to every situation. He padded to the window of the
bomb-shattered baroque mansion, one of many on the *Piazza
Cattedrale*, and peered out. The square, dominated by the
ancient cathedral, was empty save for a lone cat prowling
around the place looking for scraps. Not a policeman or an
American guard in sight. Stefan nodded his silent approval.
If the Amis and the macaroni traitors who now assisted them
intended to provide protection for this famous general of
theirs, they weren't doing it yet. As usual, only Germans
could do these things efficiently. If only for that reason, the
Anglo-American scum who had now invaded the continent
deserved to lose this war.

He dismissed the enemy from his mind and padded back
to the little hide he had made himself in the back of the big
cold room which overlooked the cathedral square. In the
thin grey moonlight which penetrated the cracks and holes
in the eighteenth-century house, he began his preparations.
One by one he took the items he needed from his sack: the
two aluminium tubes, the small compact electric battery,
the five explosive bullets, one of which alone could blow
a man's head off at 150 metres.

Swiftly but methodically he fitted the murder weapon
together. With practised fingers that needed no light to guide

them, he squeezed the smaller tube which acted as a trigger. He heard the soft hiss of compressed air. It worked. Now he loaded the bullets one by one, wiping each one thoroughly before he placed them in the breach. For this operation he wanted no stoppages. He wanted to fire and be gone in just a few seconds, for he didn't see himself as a suicide candidate. With or without the shifty little macaroni and the fat Ami, his master, he'd get back to the mainland. He'd been in trickier situations than this and survived. Then it would be a triumphant welcome by the regiment, another piece of tin, perhaps even the Knight's Cross or the Iron Cross, and then that fourteen days leave in Berlin that he had been promised, with as much gash and suds as he could stand. He smiled in the grey darkness. What a time that was going to be!

Satisfied with the weapon, he now began to move his 'hide', as he called the carefully constructed heap of bomb rubble under which he had slept, close to the glassless window from which he'd fire the fatal shot. That in place, he crawled under it once more and, placing his hands under his head, stared into nothing. All the same his mind was racing electrically as he considered the events to come.

As he saw it, the macaronis would be wandering about the place most of the day till evening when the mass would take place. They'd start to clear away as soon as the English and Americans began to appear for their own protestant church srvice; they would want little to do with the probably drunken mob of non-Catholics, except perhaps to pick their pockets and sell their sisters in the usual Sicilian fashion. He sneered at the thought.

It would be about then that the Ami military police would appear. They might check the surrounding buildings for anyone wishing any harm to their precious general, but he was prepared for that. They'd certainly have a guarded lane prepared to the doors of the cathedral where Patton would be met by the local *prominenz*. They always did such things with generals. That would mean that with a bit of luck he'd have a clear area of aim: space on both sides of the big shots with Patton moving alone at the head of his staff. He would be a perfect target.

He smiled at the thought. It wasn't a very pleasant smile, but then *Oberscharführer* Stefan Hartmann was not a very pleasant man. Satisfied he had done all he could for the time being, he made himself more comfortable in his nest and fell asleep effortlessly once more.

Mackenzie woke with a start. He hadn't slept well. He had been troubled by bad dreams. Adriana's family had appeared like evil ghosts, the mummified face of the old granny; the yellow-toothed father holding on to the neck of the donkey as if he were about to strangle it; Adriana's mother, totally naked for some inexplicable reason, long dugs hanging down to the rolls of flesh at her stomach. All of them had stared at him in eerie silence, the tears frozen on their waxen cheeks. They had stared at him with such terrifying accusation so that he when he awoke, he found himself lathered in a sticky sweat, although the dawn was cool.

Shaking a little, he didn't know why, he went over to the washbowl, which was already filled with water, and splashed some of it on his face till he was properly awake. Then he walked to the big open window and stared out at the piazza.

Slowly the city was coming to life. The first workmen were cycling to their factories; the peasants from the surrounding countryside were already setting out their wares and, over at the cafe, the fat waiter was commencing his daily routine of putting out his rickety chairs and flicking the tables with his grubby cloth. Mackenzie sniffed. It was Christmas Eve, but it didn't have the usual festive feeling associated with that day. It should have been crisp and frosty, with perhaps a touch of snow in the air. The people going about their business should have been brisk and noisy, even excited, especially the kids. For tonight they'd find presents in the stockings hung at the end of their beds, brought there by Father Christmas down the chimney.

Here the air was heavy and there was a yellow smog over the centre of the old city where the cathedral was. The people were cheerful enough and waved their arms a lot in the usual Italian fashion, but there was something lethargic about them all the same and their cheeks, instead of being bright and red, were hollowed-out and yellow, as if they had not had enough to eat for a long time.

A knock at the door. He knew it would be Sergeant Campbell. The new maid never knocked. She was a slattern who, when she bent down, deliberately revealed her hanging breasts. He knew he could have her for a packet of Players, but he felt no desire for the maid's raddled charms. Besides, an inner voice cautioned him that that wouldn't be fair to the dead girl. First he would deal with her killers before he concerned himself with his own affairs. 'Come in,' he said, a little wearily.

He had been right. It was Campbell 175. He was freshly shaved, his brasses gleamed and he had obviously gotten someone – perhaps the sloppy maid – to press his khaki drill. He clicked to attention and saluted very smartly. 'Good morning to you, sir.'

'Good morning, Sergeant,' Mackenzie replied and sat down on the rickety brass bed like an old man who had risen too quickly and now felt dizzy. 'Stand easy. You're looking very smart.'

'Last traces of the old mob, sir. Infantry, you know, sir? If it moves, salute it. If it doesn't, whitewash it. Bullshit reigns supreme sort of thing.'

Mackenzie gave him a wintry smile. What would Campbell's Jewish moneylender forefathers in the Cologne

190

ghetto think if they saw their scion now, he asked himself. Then he got on with the business of the day. 'What's the latest drill, Sergeant?'

'As of six hundred hours,' Campbell began very formally, 'we've got about a company of Yank troops on call – perhaps 120 men. Half of them will form a kind of honour for the general as he approaches the cathedral for the service. The other half will be around the Cathedral Square keeping the Eyeties in check, and any of our own lot who get pissed – excuse my French, sir – drunk, as our chaps tend to do on Christmas Eve out of respect for this festival of sweetness and light and goodwill to all men.'

Mackenzie lit a cigarette, took a drag, coughed and wished he hadn't lit the damned thing. He said, 'You're a cynic, Campbell.'

'I suppose I am, sir. A minor headache is next.'

'What?'

'I'd thought the Eyeties would steer clear of the Cathedral Square, seeing as it's a non-Catholic service and the fact that there's going to be hundreds of Anglo-American drunks in the square. I thought wrong, however. Apparently on Christmas Eve, Sicilians from other towns – Messina, Syracuse and the like – trek here to celebrate their own festivals and that of St Lucy.'

'Who's she?'

'Some alleged virgin of Roman times, sir, who wouldn't sacrifice her virginal torso to an emperor who wanted to have his wicked way with her. Being the kind of bloke who couldn't take no for an answer, he had Signora Lucy blinded with a hot iron.' He smiled winningly at his superior.

Mackenzie shook his head in mock wonder. 'As I said before, Campbell, you're a cynic. So not only will we have to deal with our own drunks, we can perhaps expect a lot of drunken Eyetie revellers as well.'

191

'Exactly, sir. However, Colonel Codman has managed to round up the whole of the island's military police force to patrol the area. So at a rough guess, we'll have some three hundred Americans on duty this afternoon and night, plus Palermo's Eyetie police force. On such a high feast day, they'll probably be drunk too. It's the nature of the beast.'

Mackenzie considered this information for a moment or two, the smoke rising from his cigarette in a slow blue spiral. Outside it was getting lighter, but no fresher. The air was still unpleasantly stuffy; perhaps they were due for a storm, Mackenzie told himself. He broke his silence. 'And that little naval deserter – Reynolds. Is he going to play ball?'

'Yessir. He's not even asking for favours. I told him what happened to the maid, Adriana,' Campbell avoided looking directly at Mackenzie, 'and that convinced him. He'll finger Joe Victory for us, if he can. And this fat US officer, if he's present today.'

'Do you think he will be, Campbell?'

'I doubt it. But he's going to have difficulty getting off the island, unless he's got some way of doing so that we don't know about.'

Mackenzie nodded his agreement. 'We're making some enquiries at Clark's HQ at Caserta. But naturally everything stops at such exalted places for Christmas, even the war. So we're not expecting much from there until after Boxing Day, I'm afraid.'

Campbell sniffed contemptuously. 'The only place where the war doesn't stop, sir, is the front. The Jerries will perhaps give us a soulful rendition of '*Stille Nacht*', but that won't stop the Nazi bastards from bumping off our boys.'

Mackenzie ignored the comment, though he knew just how true that was. 'But there is still one imponderable, Campbell,' he said thoughtfully, stubbing out the Player cigarette finally, wishing he had never lit it in the first place. Now his mouth felt like the bottom of a parrot's cage.

'What's that?'

'The missing SS man. Where does he fit into the picture, Campbell?'

Campbell scratched the back of his shaven head. 'That's a corker, sir. I can't see him working for the Yanks and trying to kill a Yankee general at same time, can you, sir?'

'No. So put it like this, Campbell. Are we looking for two separate would-be assassins working independently of each other, which would double our problems, or two working as a team?'

But at that moment, Campbell, as smart as he was, had no answer to that overwhelming question. Outside the wind had started to rise, bringing with it the sound of exploding firecrackers from far off. The St Lucy revellers from the outlying countryside were beginning to arrive . . .

Despite the early hour, the revellers from Syracuse, the place where St Lucy was martyred in the fourth century, were already well oiled. Drinking from bottles of Marsella and eating the sweet almond cakes that were always eaten on this day in honour of their patron saint, they streamed from the ancient omnibuses, most powered by gas produced in great billowing containers on the bus's roof, crying '*Santa Lucia . . . Eviva Santa Lucia!*' This drew a counter-roar from the members of the other societies descending from their own buses waving their bottles in mock anger, here and there throwing chunks of precious bread dipped in olive oil at them.

Joe Victory, standing nervously in the shadows and wearing the colours of the St Lucy Society in his buttonhole, looked at them and then at Colonel Hermann, now huddled in a GI greatcoat to hide his badges of rank.

The fat colonel's flabby face revealed nothing and the little mafioso felt he might as well be on his own for all the help he was going to receive from the colonel. At that moment he would have dearly loved to have broken away, grabbed one of the donkey carts that also mingled with the ancient buses and headed for the hills – Coreleone, somewhere like that. But he knew even that would not save him. The fat colonel and his kind had too-close links with the *famiglia* and he'd end up just another one of their *cadaveri excellente.**

'Kay,' Hermann said softly as they were swamped by the happy drunken crowd heading for the old city of Palermo, where they would undoubtedly spend the morning in bars, taking in more alcohol, getting even further into debt, before heading for the *Piazza Cattedrale*. 'You'd better get on with it. Grab yourself a bottle of the dago red those bums are drinking and join the crowd. Remember, I'm keeping my eye on you.' He touched the pocket of his GI greatcoat significantly, as if he had a pistol hidden there. 'There's got to be no slip-ups. I want to see Patton dead this day. Got it?'

'Got it,' Joe Victory echoed miserably.

'Well, get on the stick.' Hermann gave him a push and Joe Victory was propelled into the happy, noisy, drunken crowd of revellers. Moments later he had disappeared with them in the direction of the *Quattro Canti*, the 'Four Corners' where all the cheap bars were located.

Hermann breathed a sigh of relief. He had gotten the little wop off his hands for good. He'd do the job all right and he, Hermann, would ensure that it was the last thing he ever did. His connection with the Mafia thug would be finished there and then. He took out the fifth of rye whisky which was hidden in a brown paper bag, flipped open the cap and took a satisfying swig of the fiery liquid, feeling the heat burn its way down his throat. Just then a whore swayed by him on very high heels, giving him full view of her plump

*illustrious corpses.

flanks ticking back and forth like clockwork, unrestrained by any girdle or even panties. She turned and looked over her shoulder. She licked her full red lips sensuously and said, 'Looking for a good time, big boy?'

Abruptly, relieved of his problem, knowing that everything was just as Boss Krause had ordered, he felt himself overcome by lust. 'Sure, baby, I'm looking for a good time. You suck?'

The whore pursed those blood-red lips of hers and stuck out her stomach provocatively. 'GI,' she breathed, 'I do *everything*!'

Ten

Chiefie felt proud and very grateful. Now he almost swaggered as he marched down from the *Quattro Canti* to the *Piazza Cattedrale*, not paying one bit of attention to the drunken revellers who might attempt to get in his way. After all, wasn't he a chief petty officer in the King-Emperor's Royal Navy? Couldn't the Eyeties see that from his splendid new uniform, complete with two strips of medal ribbons?

He was grateful to his new bosses, Major Mackenzie and Sergeant Campbell, who had togged him out in a petty officer's white drill, starched to perfection, and trusted him not to do a bunk while he did their spotting for them. They'd even given him a small Italian pistol which he had in his right pocket. That showed they really trusted him. Indeed, Major Mackenzie had told him, just before he had set off this Christmas Eve, 'Finger the killer, Chiefie, and we'll see you get back to Blighty without a court-martial. With a bit of luck you'll be on active service within the month without a blot on your service record.'

The little cockney wasn't a sensitive man by any means, but at that moment his eyes had filled with tears and he had said in a husky voice, 'Thank you, sir. You can rely on me, sir.' And he had swung Mackenzie a tremendous salute as if he were old ABC* himself.

*Admiral A.B.C. Cunningham, chief of the Mediterranean Fleet.

Now he swaggered down the road lined with bombed-out palazzi, towards the cathedral where the Christmas Eve mass was to be held. He kept his eyes open, though he appeared to be totally unaware of the noisy Italians celebrating Santa Lucia. He knew he was supposed to be a sort of guide dog, leading the two intelligence officers who were in the cathedral square itself, to the would-be killer. But in the mood he felt now and, remembering what had happened to his crew on that lonely beach, he'd tackle the bastard personally, if needs be. He was going to show the two officers who had been so kind to him that Mrs Reynolds' handsome son was no welcher; he knew how to repay a debt.

Now as he concentrated on the buildings to the left and right and, at the same time, searched the crowds for the first sign of the potential assassin, he tried to sort out the problem which he guessed Major Mackenzie had not yet solved himself. It was the connection between the US officer, the little Eyetie rat Joe Victory and the blond killer, who he knew now – from listening carefully through the door as Mackenzie had explained it to Sergeant Campbell – was a German SS man. Why would a gang like that – a Yank, an Eyetie and a Jerry – want to kill General Patton, the Yank big shot?

A hundred yards away, the US officer who knew the answer to that particularly daunting puzzle, Colonel Hermann, was sprawled in all his naked, fat pink glory on the Sicilian whore's bed, enjoying himself, telling himself that this was the best Christmas present he had had since his prude of a wife, the pride of the Daughters of the Revolution, had allowed him to see her completely naked save for a pair of black silk panties back on Christmas Day, 1937. For between his fat legs, mottled by the red wriggling worms of bad varicose veins, the whore was going all out trying to raise his flaccid member with her cunning red tongue.

She'd do it in the end, he knew she would. She was a professional and she would be well paid for her efforts. He'd give her five dollars for her efforts, and to these wops five US greenbacks was a small fortune. So he enjoyed it, not straining to achieve an erection, just letting her work on him, savouring the hot mouth and cunning tongue labouring on his fat loins.

While she did so, he half let his mind wander. He had problems, he knew that. The most pressing was that of getting off Sicily as soon as he could. When the shit hit the fan, he wanted to be gone. He knew once he reached Caserta there'd be papers out for him immediately, posting him to Britain. There he'd be given an urgent posting to his state's own National Guard outfit with a one-star rating. Thereafter Boss Krause would take care of him. After all it would be in Boss Krause's own interest to protect him; he knew too much. And at this stage of the game, with perhaps only a year till the presidential elections, the old boy simply didn't need an embarrassing inquiry into the death of Blood an' Guts Patton.

Between his legs the whore was making noisy sucking noises and her tongue was going up and down like a fiddler's elbow. He began to feel excited. Still, he wasn't going to let himself go just yet. He was going to savour this treat to the full. Once he got back stateside, it would be Mary-Jane and her fussing about her goddam 'diafram', or whatever they called the goddam device she used as a contraceptive, and her frigging douche she used afterwards. God, Mary-Jane needed a goddam pharmacy before she'd let him make love to her and then only on a Sunday afternoon after they'd been to church . . .

Of course, he'd have to use the mass confusion that would follow Patton's death. There'd be panic at the old boy's HQ and the MPs would be whizzing around in the usual crazy circles. Cops always screwed up when the cards were down.

Perhaps he'd be able to get on to Palermo field and bum a lift back to the mainland. After all, who'd question a colonel? Rank hath its privileges.

He forgot both the whore and his chances of escape abruptly. In the distance he could hear the first muted strains of a military band. They were playing the old Sousa march, 'The Stars and Stripes for Ever'. It was the Patton Headquarters band, he knew. They were coming to perform for the crowd of drunken servicemen now beginning to gather outside the great Sicilian cathedral only yards away. They'd play until Patton made his usual grand appearance and then it would be his Seventh Army March and probably 'God Bless America'. Ole Blood an' Guts was a sucker for that kind of patriotic guff.

Now Hermann seized the whore's head and forced her mouth down further so that she choked and gasped, as if she were being strangled. He didn't care. It was time to be off, but before he went he was going to enjoy his last fling before he returned to the States and Mary-Jane. 'Come on, bitch,' he gasped through gritted teeth, the sweat now standing out on his furrowed brow like opaque pearls. 'Give it to me. *Suck!*'

Joe Victory watched the Americans as they swung into the Cathedral Square, the fat drum major swinging his mace proudly, his bandsmen blowing their instruments heartily, while the huge bass drummer slammed at his drum, as if he were trying to burst the fabric with his sticks. Here and there the assembled GIs and British sailors, most of them very drunk by now, jeered and yelled catcalls: '*Swing them arms, mate . . . Open yer legs. Nothing'll fall out . . . Bags of swank, Yanks*' and the like. But as always the the Italians were impressed by the spectacle. They cheered, waved their bottles of wine and cried, '*eviva . . . eviva*' over and over again as the band approached the cathedral, which would be soon blacked out in accordance with regulations.

Joe Victory licked his parched lips yet again. His nerves were jingling electrically. Fear and apprehension about the future had kept him on edge ever since he had left that slimy fat bastard, Colonel Hermann. It was all right for him. He was in no danger. He wasn't going to have to pull the trigger. Not that Joe Victory was – initially. For he had changed his plan to give himself the maximum chance of escaping.

Inside his right pocket he had a smoke grenade. Sicily was still full of caches of arms left by the Italian army that had surrendered there. It had been easy to obtain the grenade. As soon as Patton descended from his automobile he would throw it. In the same instant that it exploded and discharged its contents, he would push forward while the rest of the crowd backed off in fear. He would shoot Patton at close range, head for the inside of the cathedral through the main portal and go hell for leather for the *Via del Celso*, which ran parallel to the road leading up to the 'Four Corners'. From there he could disappear into the myriad streets running from the *Quattro Canti* and be gone.

Again he licked his cracked, parched lips with fear. It all sounded OK, but would it work? Some bastard might get in his way. The grenade might not explode. He made his mind stop running over the possibilities. The fact that it might go wrong didn't bear thinking about. He had to do it and that was that. Somewhere a church clock boomed six with solemn gravity. On the roof of the cathedral the lights went out one by one like those in a great theatre when the opera was about to commence. Patton was on his way. Instinctively his damp hand felt for the comforting, cold hardness of the grenade . . .

Reluctantly, George Patton prepared for the church ceremony. Meeks, his coloured servant, could see the boss was not in the mood for chat. Yet he could feel how lonely and sad Patton felt at this moment, when it seemed that his world had crashed and that his long career in the US army was about finished, so he said, 'You've got your best uniform on, General. You're gonna make them Italians' eyes pop when they see you in your finery. The boys have even relacquered your helmet.' He pointed to the gleaming helmet resting on the bed, with the three gold stars of a lieutenant-general, larger – naturally – than army regulations permitted.

Patton nodded. 'Thanks, Meeks,' he said, his voice low and spiritless. 'I guess this'll be the last Christmas I'll ever wear these duds. Civvies for me next Christmas – if I'm ever here.'

'Of course you'll be here,' said the tall black man who had served Patton so loyally over the last years. 'Believe you me, General. US darkies know about them things.'

Patton gave the sergeant a wintry smile. 'Thanks anyway, Meeks, for trying to cheer me up.' He let Meeks button up his jacket for him and then he looked at himself in the full-length mirror. For even in his misery, he was still vain. He nodded his approval at his image. 6ft 2in tall, erect, his whole outfit gleamed, from the highly polished cavalry boots to the lacquered helmet which he now placed on his greying head. He felt he looked every inch a soldier.

'All right, Meeks,' he said, finally taking his eyes off himself. 'I think that'll be all for tonight.' As an afterthought he asked, 'And what are you going to do this Christmas Eve of 1943, Meeks?'

Meeks gave him that humble smile of his. 'Well, there ain't a lot we coloured boys can do, sir,' he said carefully, 'on account of you-know-what, General.'

Patton did. The US Army was segregated. Even if it weren't, any black soldier going with a local Sicilian woman would most likely end up beaten unconscious in the gutter if any of his white 'comrades' caught him and the white woman together. 'Well, Meeks, when you grow old and have grandkids, you'll be able to tell them when they ask you what you did in the big war, that you didn't shovel shit in Louisiana!' He gave the orderly his tight yellow-toothed grin.

The orderly grinned too and then with a little bow he went out, as Colonel Codman, also dressed in his best Class A uniform complete with ribbons and pilot's wings, came in, saluted and announced, 'Everything's ready for you, sir. The automobile's waiting for you outside.' He stopped suddenly and then said, 'But sir, you're not carrying your pistols, sir.'

'We're going to church, Charley,' Patton answered. 'Not a goddam shooting gallery.'

'All the same, sir. With these killers still at large—'

'OK, OK,' Patton grumbled. 'I'll wear the goddam things. But as far as I'm concerned, Charley, the bastards can go and shoot me and get the whole goddam business over with . . .'

Mackenzie was growing ever more worried. The square in front of the great cathedral, its windows glassless, blown out by the bombing, was now in virtual darkness save where the whores flashed their torches to display their wares to the noisy, drunk, packed crowd of British sailors, American GIs and merchant seamen.

So far, Chiefie, who was wandering about the square pushing his way ruthlessly through the Allied servicemen, using the time-honoured military phrase: 'Make way there for a naval officer', had not spotted the killer; and time was running out fast. Soon the general and his entourage would be arriving and Mackenzie felt sure that the killer would make his attempt before he entered the cathedral. As he had just told an equally worried Campbell, 'If the killer makes the attempt while Patton is inside, he'll only have a limited number of escape routes. They could be soon blocked. Outside, he could make his play and then presumably duck away into the crowd. If Joe Victory has his way, that murderous swine will probably have some sort of back-up from his fellow thugs.'

Campbell had nodded his agreement, not taking his eyes off the surging, swaying crowd for one second, even from those GIs with Italian girlfriends who were attempting to jitterbug to the music of the 'Boogie-Woogie Bugle Boy of Company B', which the military band was now playing after just finishing their rendition of 'Hark the Herald Angels'.

Now Campbell said: 'Do you think I should go over and give the little fellow a hand, sir? He's just over there near that ornate lamppost. It's getting hard enough to see in this light as it is. Two pairs of eyes are better than one.'

'All right,' Mackenzie agreed hastily. 'Off you go and get through the guard of honour before the big shots arrive. I'll stay here – and keep your eyes peeled for God's sake,' he added urgently.

'Like the proverbial tinned tomato, sir,' Campbell said heartily and then he was pushing his way past a burly GI, standing motionless with his rifle at port as if he were just another of the many statues which surrounded the cathedral square.

Mackenzie turned round. Now he had his back to the guard of honour, moving his head back and forth to survey the jam-packed crowd like some intent spectator at pre-war Wimbledon. Left alone with his thoughts now, he willed himself to spot Joe Victory, for he had abruptly been seized with a burning sense of rage. It came with the thought of Adriana dead, almost before she had begun to live. Many of the young Britons and Americans who surrounded him would be dead too before next year was out. Some would survive and see old age. But Adriana had been one of those innocents caught up in a war that had really nothing to do with her, and she had paid the price for loving him in her simple peasant way. No, her life was over. She'd never see the peace and enjoy whatever benefits the end of the war might bring for its survivors, though at that moment an angry, bitter Major Mackenzie couldn't think of any in particular . . .

'Hey you,' Campbell could hear Chiefie sing out above the racket even before he reached him on the other side of the guard of honour. 'Hey you . . . *Stop*!'

He looked in Chiefie's direction. A fat man in a GI greatcoat which didn't fit him was frantically trying to push his way through the excited, drunken crowd. Instinctively he knew that this was the mysterious Yank linked with the attempt on Patton's life. Now he, too, started to push through the throng, heading for the fleeing Yank. '*Stop*!' he cried, as he pulled out his .38. 'Stop or I'll shoot.' To emphasize his threat, he raised his pistol and fired a single shot into the air.

It had an electrifying effect. Women screamed. Men shouted. Drunks dropped their bottles to the square's cobbles, where they exploded in blood-red spurts.

'*Assassenio*!' someone cried in panic. 'Murderers!' The cry was taken up on all sides. A woman fainted. Another and yet another dropped to the ground, as if they expected a full-scale shoot-out to commence at any moment. Suddenly all was chaos and panic.

Hermann panicked, too. He thrust a child out of his way, sending him screaming and reeling against the wall. He attempted to run. In his youth Chiefie had been the Home Fleet's pistol champion. He knew he was taking a chance firing at a running target in the half-light and in that crowded square. But he felt he could do it. He had to stop the fat bastard. He owed that to the two intelligence officers who had restored his pride and given him a second chance. One hand behind his back, right arm holding the pistol stretched rigid in front of him, as if he were back at pre-war Bisley, he put pressure on the trigger. He controlled his breath. Behind him, Sergeant Campbell shouted a warning. Chiefie didn't hear it. He concentrated his whole attention on the running man. He squeezed the first pressure. The pistol kicked upwards and for a fleeting second Chiefie thought he'd missed his target.

He hadn't. Suddenly, startlingly, Hermann faltered in mid-stride. His back arched like the string of a taut bow. Slowly, very slowly, his legs started to give way beneath him, as on all sides the Sicilians started to draw back, horrified at being so close to a dying man who might well put the evil eye on them.

In that same instant, its twin sirens shrieking hideously, Patton's command car turned into the square, with Patton standing imperiously in the front next to the driver like some Roman emperor of old come to upbraid his unruly subjects.

Joe Victory, a trembling bundle of nerves now, knew he could stand the strain no longer. He couldn't wait for Patton to descend from the car and join the Italian big shots. He'd have to do it now, or he'd never be able to summon up enough courage again. His hand shaking like a leaf, he drew the cotter pin out of the smoke grenade. Next instant he had thrown it in the direction of the slowing command car, reaching for his pistol already.

But Joe Victory's luck had run out. The grenade slammed against the car's bonnet, whined off the metal and a second later exploded in a burst of smoke and flashing of white phosphorus pellets on the cobbles yards away. A great cry of terror rose from the crowd. Here and there Italians reeled back screaming in agony, as the pellets struck them and began to blaze, burning away the skin and flesh immediately.

Mackenzie pulled out his pistol. 'Out of the way!' he

cried, brandishing it wildly. The crowd fell back, yelling in panic, women screaming at the tops of their voices. Suddenly there was the stench of burning flesh everywhere. Mackenzie didn't notice. He was intent on getting Joe Victory before he escaped into the milling throng.

'Stop the car!' Patton cried, reaching for his pride and joy, the symbol of his own warlike personality, his twin pistols.

The driver, panicked a little himself, instead of braking, stalled the car with a sudden jolt that sent Patton slamming into the door and winding him. He hung there momentarily, a perfect target for the killer.

Joe Victory knew it was his last chance. He snapped off the safety catch and flung up the pistol. In the light of the burning victims of his grenade, writhing and twisting frantically on the cobbles, trying to put out those grey, flesh-eating pellets of phosphorus, he aimed at the general still slumped over the side of the command car, trying desperately to draw out his pistols and save himself. Suddenly he felt the adrenalin surging through his skinny frame. With it came renewed confidence. It wouldn't be the first time he had killed a man. He had made his first bones back as a sixteen-year-old kid in New York's Bronx. He'd shot a renegade cop on the take, who would not deliver when the *capo* had asked him for a favour. He'd walked right up to him and pressed his piece into the cop's fat guts and had blasted him in ten different ways. There had been blood and snot flying everywhere. Now he was going to do it again.

But Major Mackenzie was quicker. He hadn't time to take aim so that he didn't hit the general. He fired low. The bullet hit Joe Victory in the right leg. The limb disintegrated in a welter of blood and smashed bone. Joe Victory screamed with the unbearable pain. The pistol tumbled from his suddenly nerveless fingers and he stumbled to the ground helplessly.

Mackenzie didn't give him a chance. Why should he? The

bastard had killed Adriana, that poor innocent kid. Now it was his turn. He fired. Joe Victory's body twitched violently as the slug slammed into him at such close range. He yelled something. Mackenzie didn't understand – didn't care. He was consumed by a cold unreasoning rage, the primeval bloodlust to kill. He bent down as Joe Victory lay there helplessly on the bloodstained cobbles, dying by the second. He had evacuated his bowels. He stank. Mackenzie didn't notice. All he wanted now was to put an end to the runt's life. Coldly, almost clinically, though inside an icy fury raged, he placed the muzzle of his big .38 at the base of the dying man's skull just behind his right ear and pulled the trigger for the last time . . .

Up in his hiding place in the second storey of the ruined building, Stefan had viewed the violent events below dispassionately. In the light of the burning bodies he could see what was happenning some seventy metres away quite clearly. Now he waited to check whether the Ami general who had been thrown against the side of his vehicle had been hit or not. He cared nothing about the fact that Ami soldiers and MPs were running about all over the place. There was even one tall policeman in his white-painted helmet spraying the building in which he found himself with tommy-gun fire, for no particular reason. It didn't worry him. He'd fought the Amis in Italy. He knew they always over-reacted, even panicked, when things went wrong for them. Even the splinters of stone and chippings that flew through the glassless window didn't disturb his concentration. He smiled contemptuously. Now he'd show them. He waited.

Slowly Patton rose.

Stefan drew in his breath sharply. The macaroni had missed. The Ami general was still alive. Now it was up to him. Calmly he raised the little electric-powered rifle which could kill silently, an attribute which had first brought it to the attention of the *Abwehr*, the German secret service. Not that Stefan's thoughts were on the Berlin secret service at that moment. His loyalty was first and foremost to *Wotan*, his old regiment. What a distinction it would be for the premier regiment of the SS elite if one of its members killed the Ami commander who had won the battle for Sicily and forced the *Wehrmacht* into retreat up the boot of Italy.

Carefully he centred the sight on the old Ami general outlined by the flickering white light of the phosphorus victims, still writhing on the ground all around. It was going to be almost too easy, he told himself, as the cross in the gun's sight dissected Patton's head. Down on the first storey there was the sound of another salvo ripping the length of the building. Stefan didn't even notice. His whole being was concentrated on the imminent murder of the Ami general. He must not let anything distract him now from his overwhelming task.

He took first pressure, forcing himself to breathe steadily and calmly. His first bullet must do it, for each of his special slugs had to be loaded into his strange little rifle individually, and that took time. '*One*,' he counted off to himself, slightly increasing the pressure on the trigger. '*Two* . . .' His breathing was totally under control now. The butt of the little rifle was snug and tight into his right shoulder, as if he and the weapon had become one. '*Three!*'

The sudden burst of blinding white light from the command car's spotlight directed upwards caught him completely and totally by surprise, blinding him with its harsh glare in the very instant that he took final pressure on the trigger. He felt the rifle kick him in the shoulder and even as it did so, he knew that he had missed his target.

Turning his head to one side, he reloaded as swiftly as he could. He knew he still had a chance to hit Patton. Old men took time to recover. '*Boshe moi*,' he cursed in Russian to himself. '*Davoi!*' The light swept the interior of the bombed upper story. '*Move it!*'

Down below, Mackenzie yelled at the top of his voice. 'Keep that building under fire, you idiots . . . keep bloody firing!' He started to blaze away with his own revolver.

A handful of yards away, Colonel Codman attempted to throw himself over the general to protect him, crying urgently, 'Keep down, sir . . . Oh for God's sake, *keep down!*'

As the big MP sergeant with the tommy-gun opened up again, ripping a burst the length of the building opposite, sending stone chippings and mortar flying in a grey mist, Patton pushed Codman away. 'Like hell will I keep down. I've never dodged fire in my whole goddam life. Let me get at the murdering bastard.' Even as Codman reached out to stop him, Patton had whipped out his twin pistols like some Western gunslinger in a Hollywood B movie . . .

Breathing a little more sharply now, Stefan rammed home the bullet, twisted the bolt and raised himself to get a better view of his target below. He was not afraid of the machine-gun bullets rattling and whining off the wall of the bombed building. He'd been under fire enough with *Wotan* to know that the firer was panicked. He wasn't aiming. He was just firing totally wildly in the hope he'd hit *something*. He grinned, baring his teeth like a wolf about to pounce.

Below, the spotlight had moved. He narrowed his eyes, getting accustomed to the new light. Imprinted on his retina was the stark black outline of the general standing boldly upright. His wolfish grin broadened. '*Auf wiedersehen,* Ami—' he began. His final parting shot ended suddenly in a cry of agony. Something had struck him on the shoulder and penetrated into the hard flesh like the tip of a red-hot poker. He gasped. The little rifle was beginning to droop. He hadn't the strength to hold it. Desperately, as that dark erect figure wavered and trembled before his gaze, distorted as if seen through a mist, he tried to keep the rifle on target. To no avail. He was losing control of his body. But he had to kill Patton, come what may. '*Kill!*' he ordered himself through gritted teeth. '*Kill him . . . you must . . .*' As if it was the most important thing he had ever done in this life, Stefan tried yet again to raise the rifle. The sweat stood out in opaque beads on his brow. The little weapon seemed to weigh a ton. But he was doing it . . . He was . . .

The second shot caught him squarely in the centre of his distorted sweat-glazed face. In an instant his features were transformed grotesquely. They looked as if someone had thrown thick red jam at them. The scream of absolute pain died in his throat. He slammed backwards against the opposite wall, dead before he hit it.

Eleven

MESSAGE TO CG 7th ARMY FOR PATTON,
22 JANUARY 1944, GEORGE S. PATTON JR.
LIEUTENANT-GENERAL, 02605, US ARMY.
　ORDERS ISSUED RELIEVING YOU FROM
ASSIGNMENT IN THIS THEATRE AND ASSIGN-
ING TO DUTY IN UK. REQUEST YOU PROCEED
TO NATOUSA, ALGIERS, FOR ORDERS.

Ole Blood an' Guts Patton's days of glory were about to
recommence.

ENVOI

A t precisely nine o'clock that December day of 1945, the funeral ceremony commenced. As the train bearing the general's coffin drew into the *Gare de Luxembourg*, the guard of honour from his beloved Third US Army snapped to attention. Behind the ramrod-straight GIs, soldiers of other Allied formations did the same. Immediately the Luxembourg military band started to play 'Sonnerie aux Morts' with great pomp and solemnity. The dead general, lying in full uniform in his metal coffin, would have loved it.

Behind the coffin came the dead general's wife, entirely in black, and some of his divisional and corps commanders, who weren't ashamed to be seen in Luxembourg City this grey, drizzly day. Exactly two years before, on December 24th, 1943, the dead general had been in disgrace in far away Sicily. Now on *this* Christmas Eve he was in disgrace again.

Hence none of the top brass – Eisenhower, Bradley, Clark – for whom the dead general and the men of his beloved Third Army had secured their victory, had thought it politic to attend this last ceremony. As Lieutenant Campbell, MM, standing with the other Allied officers, a black band around his upper arm, whispered to Colonel Mackenzie, DSO, MC, as the cortege neared the gun carriage which would bear the dead general's coffin to Hamm cemetery, where 6,000 of his dead soldiers lay: 'The top brass won't want to be associated with such an old reprobate, Colonel, especially now, when

215

they say Eisenhower might run for president. The voters in the USA might not like it.'

Mackenzie, more sombre and withdrawn than ever these days, nodded and said, 'Ironic, isn't it? They attempted to kill the old boy back then because he posed a threat to their other presidential hopefuls. Some say the accident* which killed him in Germany wasn't an accident either; the old boy knew too much – and now Ike's running for president.' He shrugged as Master-Sergeant Meeks, his face yellow with the biting cold, stepped forward at the head of the other pallbearers. 'Crazy world.'

Campbell nodded. It was. Back in Sicily when he had first joined Mackenzie, Britain had still been top dog, the senior partner in the Anglo-American coalition. Now Britain and the British Empire, of which the one-time German Jew was inordinately proud, were on their way out. Churchill had gone, Britain was broke and the new government seemed only too eager to get rid of the Empire. Now America was the new world super power. From this time onwards, Britain – 'little England', as Campbell 175 called it – would have to dance to the Yanks' tune.

Now the pallbearers placed the coffin on to the gun carriage. The Luxembourg military band struck up the US national anthem. The Allied officers snapped to attention. The many Luxembourgers watching, who regarded Patton as their liberator, took off their hats in respect. Here and there a woman sobbed. Slowly as the strains of the anthem died away, the carriage began to roll, escorted by outriders on their motorbikes.

*Patton had been severely injured in a slight motor accident while on his way to go hunting. He appeared to recover, then died abruptly in a US hospital in Heidelberg, Germany. Some rumours had it at the time that in reality Patton had been murdered because he had threatened to resign from the US Army in January 1946 and 'tell all'.

It was a solemn scene and Mackenzie, as hardbitten and as cynical as he had become, was moved. He let his arm fall and said to Campbell. 'I didn't like him, you know. He stood for a lot of things I detested. But in his way, he was a great man – a great soldier. I don't think we'll see his like again soon.'

Campbell didn't comment. He had his own thoughts on Patton, the dead general now on his way to be buried in this foreign soil. For Patton had insisted before his death that he should be buried among his fighting soldiers and not in his native earth. Instead, Campbell asked, 'Are we going to the cemetery, Colonel?'

'No, Campbell,' Mackenzie answered. 'We've seen enough dead in these last terrible years. Undoubtedly we'll see more before long. No, I need a drink. Let's find a bar instead.'

Campbell 175 was about to protest that it was just after nine o'clock in the morning, but thought better of it. 'Yes, that sounds a good idea to me, sir. Let's find a bar.'

Together they turned and gently forced their way through the sombre crowd of civilians. Moments later they had disappeared. Behind them the gun carriage, bearing the dead general, headed for the final parade, accompanied by the solemn beat of a drum. It was all over. History had reached out and embraced George S. Patton at last.

.